Max Lobe was born in Douala, Cameroon. At eigh[illegible] he moved to Switzerland, where he earned a BA in communication and journalism and a Master's in public policy and administration. In 2017, his novel *Confidences* won the Ahmadou Kourouma Prize. *A Long Way From Douala* was published to rave reviews in French in 2018 and in 2021 in English. Max Lobe lives in Geneva.

Ros Schwartz is an award-winning translator of more than 100 works of fiction and non-fiction, including the 2010 edition of Antoine de Saint-Exupéry's *The Little Prince.* Among the Francophone authors she has translated are Tahar Ben Jelloun, Aziz Chouaki, Fatou Diome, Dominique Eddé and Ousmane Sembène. In 2009, she was made a Chevalier de l'Ordre des Arts et des Lettres, and in 2017 she was awarded the John Sykes Memorial Prize for Excellence.

Max Lobe was born in Douala, Cameroon. At eighteen he moved to Switzerland, where he earned a BA in communication and journalism and a Master's in public policy and administration. In 2017, his novel *Confidences* won the Ahmadou Kourouma Prize. *A Long Way From Douala* was published to rave reviews in French in 2018 and in 2021 in English. Max Lobe lives in Geneva.

Ros Schwartz is an award-winning translator of more than 100 works of fiction and non-fiction, including the 2010 edition of Antoine de Saint-Exupéry's *The Little Prince*. Among the francophone authors she has translated are Tahar Ben Jelloun, Aziz Chouaki, Fatou Diome, Dominique Eddé and Ousmane Sembène. In 2009 she was made a Chevalier de l'Ordre des Arts et des Lettres and in 2017 she was awarded the John Sykes Memorial Prize for Excellence.

DOES SNOW TURN A PERSON WHITE INSIDE?

MAX LOBE

Translated by

Ros Schwartz

SMALL AXES

HopeRoad Publishing
PO Box 55544
Exhibition Road
London SW7 2DB
www.hoperoadpublishing.com
@hoperoadpublish

First published as *La Trinité bantoue*

Published by arrangement with Agence Litteraire Astier-Pécher

This edition first published in 2022 by Small Axes, an imprint of HopeRoad

A CIP catalogue record for this book is available from the British Library

ISBN: 978-1-913109-90-5

eISBN: 978-1-913109-96-7

swiss arts council
prohelvetia

Printed and bound by Clays Ltd, Elcograf S.p.A

For my mother and best friend, Chandèze

Ah Sita, lè Nyambè a te ki wè nin

1

I've been stuck up here on a big hill above Lugano for almost half an hour, desperately waiting for a bus that's not coming. The sun's at its height and is beating down on my shaved head, my kongolibon.

There's an old lady near me. She's wearing an elegant cream-coloured dress. Her long white hair sweeps her bare shoulders. It's so hot that her foundation has run, exposing the fine lines around her eyes. This lady talks non-stop. She moans. She grumbles. She must be complaining about this outrageous public transport delay. And saying that they keep putting the fares up. I *think* I understand – she's speaking in Italian. I smile at her without even knowing why. Actually, I can't grasp much of this language. Just snatches I can make out in passing. But as my sister Kosambela always says, French and Italian are a bit like the Bantus and the Swiss: distant cousins, perhaps even close. All of a sudden, I can understand a tiny fraction of what the old lady is on about.

Across the road is a bus shelter for public transport vehicles going in the opposite direction from the one I'm waiting for. There are two youths there. Like us, their patience is running out. They look exasperated. A man in a sweat-soaked white vest trundles past with an orange wheelbarrow bearing the town's logo. It's a wheelbarrow belonging to the municipal highways department. Whistling, the man empties the bins. That at least, the look on the old lady's face seems to say. She's still beside me, complaining endlessly.

A poster close to the bin-man catches my eye. It shows three white sheep in a peaceful meadow – a red background with a white cross. One of the white sheep, smiling, is kicking out with its hind legs against a black sheep. On the poster are the words *creare sicurezza*.

I calmly have a smoke and contemplate the poster. The image strikes me as quite funny. Then I recall how the expression 'black sheep' was a favourite of my father, who was a soldier in Bantuland's regular army. As well as black sheep, he would very often say: you KGB (for spy), or Senegalese honker or motormouth (for someone who was a chatterbox). When there was talk of traitors in the army ranks, or weaklings, or those killed in battle, my father always used to say jubilantly: they're just black sheep!

The big bell of a distant church begins to toll. I realise that I've been waiting for my bus for nearly three quarters of an hour. At another time in my life, not so long ago in fact, I'd have taken a taxi. That's what another lady did – no way was she prepared to hang around for more than five minutes. But the thing is, just over a year ago, as I was heroically finishing my Master's, I learned that I had lost my job.

I was a travelling sales rep for Nkamba African Beauty. After nearly five years of dedicated and loyal service, my boss, Monsieur Nkamba, let me go. He did so without any qualms. He gave no real explanation. That was that, period: he was terminating our collaboration. Besides, we had no written contract. I sold his products and he paid me my gombo. It was all hush-hush. Between ourselves. Between us brothers from Bantuland. What am I saying? Nkamba was only originally from there. Because only a few months ago, he went over to the other side. He had proudly given up his Bantu citizenship and become Swiss. Exclusively Swiss. I'm a true-true *Eidgenosse*, I am! he would say, puffing out his chest. I've even heard that he voted for the far right. But I couldn't care less about that. The most important thing for me was my job. And now I don't have one.

When Monsieur Nkamba told me he no longer wanted me, I couldn't believe it. What was I accused of? What could he accuse me of? I made money for him. Very good money, even. I'd never pocketed anything. I'd never acted inappropriately towards his female customers. Quite the opposite, we had excellent business relations. I had never misbehaved either towards him or towards anyone in that dodgy business, selling goods that entered the country fraudulently. I'd never refused to carry out the slightest errand. I wasn't just his sales rep, but also his dogsbody. *Mwana, can you go and pick up my sons from school? Mwana, can you go and collect my suit from the dry cleaners? Mwana, can you do this or that?* And even, *Mwana, don't you know any pretty girls you can introduce me to?* Then he'd add, stroking his belly that's even bigger than that of a heavily pregnant woman: *a man can't eat rice every day, you understand that, don't you?*

I was faithful and loyal to him. But he had no qualms about booting me out.

I begged him. I had no choice: that job was my livelihood. It enabled me to pay for my studies, to meet my needs and even to send a little gombo to Monga Minga, my mother, back in Bantuland. Monsieur Nkamba didn't pay any social security contributions and I didn't pay any tax. That was our agreement. That way, all the gombo I earned went straight into my pocket, my stomach and, more recently, that of my Ruedi too.

There's no point arguing, Monsieur Nkamba had said, caressing his fat, gold-ringed fingers. No compassion. Without saying goodbye, I walked out of his office that was too cramped for his colossal girth. I slammed the door so hard that all the contempt and disdain I now felt for him rang out in a loud thunderclap.

I haven't seen Monsieur Nkamba since.

Now, I regret having left him in that way. Maybe I should have carried on begging. Maybe he would have listened to my pleas in the end. Maybe he'd have remembered our excellent working relationship of almost five years. Maybe I should even have suggested renegotiating our contract, reducing my salary, giving up my bonus on sales of his imitation products. Maybe I should have threatened to report him to the Swiss authorities. Maybe . . .

While I'm waiting for the bus, it's not the business with Nkamba African Beauty that's bothering me.

Monsieur Nkamba made his choice. And sooner or later, I'm bound to find a proper job worthy of my skills, I tell myself with a slender conviction that seeps from my shaven head.

It's not the wait for the bus that's bothering me. We're in the habit of saying about our distant cousins that they are people of impeccable punctuality. Yes, but it can happen that they are late – and very late, even them. It's not the old lady's anger that's bothering me: she can moan all she likes, she'll still have to wait for this delayed fucking bus. It's not even that political poster plastered opposite – whose vile message that some found so offensive I would only understand weeks later – that's bothering me. No. It's not even my red Louboutins that I'd proudly bought myself at the time when things were going well. What concerns me the most right now is these two Mbanjoks I'm lugging! Two huge sugar-cane bags, each weighing at least thirty kilos.

What's in them? Food! Oh yes! Food and nothing else. Direct from Bantuland.

2

Two months ago, my sister Kosambela decided to show her homeland to her sons, two beautiful mixed-race kids aged eight and six, with frizzy hair and full lips. She'd always wanted to do this, and no one, not even a bulldozer, could have got the idea out of her head.

In Bantuland she was going to make men of those two little Western wimps. Real men. No way were they going to turn out like their father, what's-his-name, who's not ashamed to do the household chores and even wanted to take paternity leave to be the children's primary carer. He cries when he tells his wife he loves her! He cries because one of his sons is sulking and won't eat his supper. Worse, he cries because he hasn't heard from his mother for two weeks. That kind of behaviour alarmed my sister. She'd think about our soldier father and exclaim: is he a man? He's a black sheep! And if it hadn't been for that thing – yes, that's what my sister called her husband: 'that thing' – she, Kosambela Matatizo in person, should already have dragged her boys off to Africa, to Bantuland, a long time ago. But now, as I'm speaking to you, she can do it because there's no longer a husband in the house. She's raising her kids on her own.

When Kosambela had told me about their trip to Bantuland, to the M'fang region, northwest of where we come from, I did a little dance to show how thrilled I was. I could picture my nephews being overwhelmed by the vastness and beauty of that country populated by extraordinary people. I'd asked Kosambela not to forget to show them the Victoria Falls, the Lobé Falls and the Mosi-oa-Tunya national park. I asked her to take them to the Katanga Hills, the shores of Lake Tanganyika, to the top of Mount Kilimanjaro and Mount Fako, not forgetting the Limpopo and Ubangi rivers, the elephants in the Okavango Delta and the zebra in the Etosha national park – and that was just for starters.

Then, joy gave way to fear. I was sick with worry for the boys. Poor things, I thought. How would they react to the sad reality of our urban landscapes and the weight of our traditions that were unheard of here in Switzerland, their birthplace? Would they be traumatised? Would they be able to cope? I immediately drew Kosambela's attention to all the health issues, especially vaccinations:

'They absolutely must have all the vaccinations. And I mean all.'

'We'll do what we can, by the grace of Nzambe. He alone protects us.'

She'd carried on telling her white prayer beads, which never left her side, even when she called her husband 'that thing'. She'd paused for thought, as if asking Nzambe for the right answer. Then, abruptly, she turned to me.

'My sons have true black blood in their veins.'

'Black blood? Where have you heard that black blood protects against malaria or typhoid?'

'*Fratellino,*' she laughed, still telling her beads, 'the mosquitoes know who to bite. So, drop the subject.'

Thinking back, I'm sure Kosambela was making fun of me. I think she ended up getting all the vaccinations for her sons. I also think that she did everything necessary to prevent them from being bitten by a nasty female mozzie, curious to taste a new type of blood, mixed blood, a blood cocktail. Cheers! In any case, the kids came back safe and sound – and circumcised, of course. Praise be to Nzambe! my mother said on the phone.

My mother, in Bantuland, apparently, had been shocked on seeing the photos of me, which Kosambela had shown her. My mother found I had grown very thin.

'Oh Nzambe!' she'd exclaimed. '*C'est quoi comme ça là?* What is that, he looks like a desert mosquito. Is he starving to death over there or what?'

'You know,' my sister had replied, 'life among the Whites is very tough.'

'I'm sure it's the lady from the job centre who's eating him up like that. Is she trying to kill my child or what? Or is it the food over there that doesn't agree with him?'

'We must keep praying.'

'God helps those who help themselves,' my mother concluded.

And so, Monga Minga decided to help herself so that God would come to her aid. She took drastic steps to remedy this problem. And quickly. No way was she going to let her child die without doing anything. So, she made up her mind to send me lots and lots of food from back home: ndoleh. Oh, delicious ndoleh! My mother chooses randomly. She knows how much I love those vegetables! Fumbwa, saka-saka, makayabu, okra and dried impwa. Boiled peanuts, grilled peanuts, dried peanuts, caramelised peanuts, peanut oil, peanut butter, peanuts and more peanuts. Cassava bobolos, cassava powder, cassava doughnuts, tapioca, savoury cassava pancakes, cassava and more cassava. Pumpkin-seed cake, black-eyed pea cakes, coconut cakes, cakes and more cakes. Taro, macabo. Palm oil, dried bush meat and so on, and so on. Awesome, really awesome. Everything needed to fatten up her Bantu foal in Switzerland. My mother is no fool. She'd made all those food choices because she knew very well that the mouth that has suckled never forgets the taste of milk.

She had carefully wrapped all my provisions, first in cling film, then in aluminium foil, and then newspaper, and then in big Mbanjok sacks. My mother had frozen them for several days. Kosambela had dutifully kept them frozen at her place, as soon as she returned to Lugano.

And now the bus's delay was going to fuck it all up. All my precious provisions were likely to melt like margarine in the sun. *Cioè!*

At long last, the bus arrives. It's nearly an hour overdue. I pull a face and let out a long tsssss! before boarding. With a wet wipe, I dab at the drops of sweat beading on my head. The aircon cools my burning kongolibon. It feels good. The old lady carries on railing against the delays, public transport and, and, and . . . They bring shame on this country for nothing, she's probably saying on a loop. Me too, I'm annoyed, especially because I've got another six hours' journey ahead of me until I reach Geneva, on the other side of the country. The trains are slow on this route and I'll have to pray to Nzambe that my provisions will remain intact until I reach home.

In the bus, I stare at the driver whose face I can see in the rear-view mirror. He's stocky and bearded. I wonder whether his feet reach the pedals of his vehicle. I put my bags out of reach of any thieving hands. What will Ruedi, my Alpine fox, say when he sees such a mountain of food from Africa? Because I know him so well, I know that he'll smile at me first. He'll be guarded. Then he'll ask me if the donations from the World Food Programme have gone to the wrong address. We'll both laugh. We'll make more jokes about it. And ultimately, his Cartesian European mind will very quickly take over. And then, I'm convinced he'll say: but Mwana, you know, we haven't got room for all that in our little fridge.

3

Here in the land of my distant cousins, today's the national holiday. But it is in Bantuland as well. God only knows why these two countries, which in theory have nothing in common, have chosen the same date for their national holiday. In Switzerland, the first of August is the anniversary of a certain oath taken by three gentlemen, representing the very first cantons of the Swiss heartland. They call it the Grütli Oath. It's said to have been signed at the end of the thirteenth century. Some – generally very elitist people – say that it's a myth rather than the real truth. They say that it's a nice little story for children. For children who still want to believe in it, that is. Others however, their chests thrust out, say that it is the very foundation of the country. Of its strength. Between these two visions of their national holiday, I'm not someone, poor little Bantu that I am, who's going to judge.

When I tell the story and the anti-story of the Swiss Grütli Oath to Monga Minga, she makes no secret of her surprise, her emotion. Those people are so far in advance of us, she says over the phone. They were already signing pacts in those long-ago times? she asks. Then she adds, with a heavy note of irony in her voice, in those long-ago times, we were still walking barefoot in the forest among the animals.

We laugh. We're making fun of ourselves.

Ruedi isn't there. He's gone off to his native Grison Alps. He decided to go there because he doesn't want to eat ndoleh, even less pundu. He pooh-poohs the food from Bantuland, that guy. He hasn't told me so in his own words. But after two long years of living together, we don't necessarily need to spell things out to understand each other.

As he was leaving the apartment, he invited me to go with him. He was being a smart-arse. He knew very well that I'd never accept his invitation, because I was entertaining Dominique at our place. And when either of us is entertaining Dominique, he needs time to devote to him. We'd rarely entertained him together. Each time one of us, Ruedi or I, had to disappear, we'd leave the other one with Dominique. Over time, we ended up giving him his own place in our lives. He has a spare key. He knows that if we're not there, he can go into our apartment. Because it's also his place. But I doubt he will. He'll always wait for one of us to be home. He'll wait for one of us to invite him. And then he'll leave his apartment in Carouge and come over to ours.

The weather's been very hot these past few days. People are talking of nothing but the heatwave. They come out with the usual seasonal advice: drink plenty of water, don't stay out in the sun for too long, avoid physical exercise when the sun's high in the sky. For a few days, I've been doing my best to follow these recommendations.

At midday, I lower the blinds in my bedroom to keep it cool. Then, when evening comes, I open all the windows to let in the fresh air from the lake. That's what I plan to do later when I get out of bed. I'm still lying there. I've just woken up. Dominique's gone. I'd fallen into a deep, blissed-out sleep.

He left me a note on the kitchen table before going off. He says that he'd been happy to see me again. He says that it was good. Very good, even. I smile. Pity, he adds, he'd have liked to see Ruedi too. At the end of his note, he wishes me a happy national Bantu holiday. See you soon, he signs off.

I rub my eyes, still puffy with sleep. I crumple his note and throw it in the kitchen bin on top of the banana leaves that had been wrapped around the cassava bobolos that I'd been pigging out on all day.

I open the bedroom windows and stand there to have a smoke. I look at the apartment block opposite. It's decked out. At almost every window, there's a red flag with a white cross. But not only one flag. There are also lots of flags from other countries: Italy, Portugal, Spain, Albania, Kosovo, France, Germany and so on. But I can't see any from Africa, even less from Bantuland. And yet, the neighbourhood is very multicultural. Then I think of my Bantu flag – yes, I do have one. I'd brought it with me when I left the country. That was a long time ago. I'd placed it on the very top of my belongings. Then I'd closed the suitcase. I did so with a certain pride, which I still recall today: the pride of an ambassador who has the honour of representing his country abroad. But since then, that pride has dwindled. My flag's lying in some rathole somewhere. Why have I never hung my flag at my window as others do? Am I not proud enough of my country to do so? Could I be ashamed to say where I come from? At the home of my former boss and fellow Bantuland countryman, the Swiss and Genevan flags greeted you in the hallway of the house he'd bought in the Geneva countryside. You can't get any more Genevan than him.

I feel a pang of guilt. To shrug it off, I think of Ruedi. I tell myself he must be smoking on the terrace of a bar perched on the hills overlooking his valley. I think of Kosambela who, at this hour, must still be at a federal prayer gathering somewhere. I think of the inevitable military parades that celebrate the pride of the Bantu on the first of August. It's not just the army, the police or the remnants of the fire brigade at this procession: schoolchildren, students and our numerous political parties also take part. The only major absentees are the ambulance crews. It's not that they boycott the national day parade, it's that this service simply doesn't exist in Bantuland. It no longer exists.

Still at my bedroom window, my face caressed by the cool breeze coming off Lake Geneva, I think about the rainy season in Bantuland, which is such a strong contrast to the heatwave here. A rainy season that brings with it a regiment of tenacious mosquitoes armed to the teeth, ready to drain you of your blood. Memories of mosquitoes spring up in my mind. I remember Kosambela telling me, when she was little, that you had to be careful of the Bantuland mosquitoes. Yes, because according to her, they weren't ordinary mosquitoes. They were sorcerer mosquitoes! she claimed earnestly. She said that even anti-mosquito spray couldn't kill them because they whacked on a gas mask before coming to suck your blood while you were asleep. Black sheep, I'd say to my sister then, trying to imitate our father's authoritarian voice. Kosambela was convinced that the only way to drive those mosquitoes from Bantuland was to attack them head-on with a hammer, or better, a rake. When I think back to all those moments of our childhood, I smile.

I phone Ruedi.

'So, have you eaten something different?' I ask him.

'Grilled meat. Lots of grilled meat. What about you?'

'You know. The same.'

I hear him smile. I don't know whether he's making fun of me or whether it's because he's pleased, on this Swiss national holiday, not to be eating Bantu food.

'What about Dominique?' he asks. 'Was it good?'

'As always. Very good.'

Ruedi says nothing for a moment. The smile I heard a few seconds earlier fades. I don't know why. Perhaps he'd like me to go into more detail about what happened with Dominique? Perhaps he'd like more time to decipher my laconic reply? I'm a bit surprised because there are no secrets when it comes to Dominique. I keep quiet. Since I say nothing more, Ruedi starts speaking again and tells me how he's spent the national holiday.

He says that he and his family went to Grütli Meadow. That first they sailed from the banks of the Flüelen, across Lake Lucerne, on a motorboat that his father had hired. That the sun was beating down so hard that they had to stop a few times to swim in the cool water of the lake. That once there, at the famous Grütli Meadow, the very one where the Swiss Oath had been signed at the end of the thirteenth century while we Bantus were still walking barefoot in the forest among the animals, there were a lot of people. That's only to be expected on the national holiday. That lush meadow surrounded by snow-capped mountains all year round is coveted by the politicians of all stripes. Each political party wants to claim its share of the Grütli. Each one wants to rewrite the story of the so-called founding pact. Ruedi says that the President of the Confederation gave a speech in front of a crowd in red and white. He says that suddenly, people dressed in black with heads as clean-shaven as mine appeared. He even used the word kongolibon to describe their hairstyle, which makes me laugh. He says they started making a great din and disturbed the peace and quiet of the legendary meadow. That the police stepped in rapidly to calm things down. After all, it was only to be expected. He says that, luckily, order was quickly restored. That later, there was an excellent brunch.

That—

'Have you asked your parents for money?' I break in sharply.

'I'm going to.'

'Ruedi!'

'Promise.'

'Bring some food back with you too.'

'Have you already finished your grub from home?'

Ruedi laughs. I ask him to bring back some food so he won't starve to death from refusing to eat what comes from my country. Because I can manage with all that Monga Minga has sent me. But for how long?

4

Hell has been banging hard at our door for some time. I still haven't found my dream job, or even a job full stop. And despite all my efforts, I haven't seen any portents boding a real change, *cioè* a real job corresponding to my great expectations as a young graduate. All our savings have run out. Ruedi brought back from his native mountains a paltry little gombo that enabled us to pay the rent and a few other bills. We just about managed to keep our heads above water this month. Otherwise, we don't have much left. Almost nothing, apart from the food that came from Bantuland.

In my hand is all the cash I've collected that was lying around our apartment. A few forgotten coins in a drawer, a jeans pocket or under the bed. A lot of yellow coins – the ones no one wants to have in their pocket, the ones that even the vagrants and beggars reserve the right to refuse.

As if to negotiate sharing out an inheritance of billions, we confer at length to decide what to do with our fortune, stacked up in front of us.

'Eleven francs thirty-five,' I say, looking at the pile of small change on our little kitchen table.

Ruedi rolls a cigarette with typical precision. He lights it and blows out a thick, yellowish smoke which obscures his purple face.

'What are we going to eat in the coming days?' he asks, and I can sense all the anxiety lurking in his throat.

'There's still some ndoleh left. We haven't eaten it all. There's also some cassava and peanut soup, and a few pumpkin-seed cakes. That ought to do.' Ruedi reddens. I can see that he doesn't know what to say. He's out of his depth. As we sit there, if he opens his mouth, he's going to feel so sorry about our predicament that he's going to start blubbing like a kid abandoned by his mother. And if I open my mouth, I might suggest drastic austerity measures that will make him cry just as hard. But I don't want him to cry. And anyway, he has no real reason to complain – I've just landed a little three-month work placement that will keep us afloat for a while. That's a good start. At least it means I will have some news for my adviser from the unemployment office who can't do anything for me in any case.

'Go on, have a smoke,' I say to Ruedi. 'It'll blow over. We'll get through this. Come on!'

'Since when did *you* believe in miracles?'

'Nzambe only made a rough cast of man. It's here on earth that each person creates themselves.'

'Another of your stupid proverbs.'

A long silence follows. I stare out of the window and notice once again the flags adorning the apartment building opposite that remind me of my own, which I conceal beneath my unavowed shame.

'It'll be fine,' I say. 'I know it will. It'll be fine. We just have to fight.'

'Do you really think we'll be able to hold out until you get your first pay cheque, at the end of September? That's a good four weeks away. Do you see what I mean? Four weeks!'

'What's certain is that we won't die of hunger. You'll just have to start eating saka-saka and cassava bobolos.'

'Who? Me?'

'Bah, who else?'

'But . . .'

'But what? Hey, I eat fondue and rösti, don't I?'

Ruedi hangs his head. My argument may not be so obvious, but it is valid. Now, my companion doesn't know what else to say. The silence merges with the smoke and creates a strange atmosphere in the room. Ruedi seems overwhelmed by the situation. He turns his gaze to the pile of coins. He stares at them, studies them. I wonder what he's looking for in that pile. At any rate, he'll see no more than all the shit that's happening to us. I'm waiting for him to say whether he sees anything other than poverty. But he remains silent. His hollow cheeks turn a deeper shade of purple. On his face, I read something that could be defeat, failure, but also bitterness or self-pity.

How could he, Ruedi, the only son of the highly venerable Baumgartner family, find himself in such circumstances? Do his parents know? Last time he saw them at the Grütli Meadow, did he screw up the courage to tell them the whole truth about his situation, about our situation? I don't think so.

Ruedi says he doesn't like to ask. Especially not his parents. He doesn't want them to help us out. He says he doesn't want to bother anyone. A few weeks ago, just before he went to his parents' place for the national holiday, he told me, not without a certain pride, of his refusal to ask his parents for money. The very rare times when they had given us a little gombo, were the times when I put so much pressure on Ruedi that he eventually gave in. On these occasions, his parents smiled as they handed him an envelope. They seemed glad to be able to help us out. They told us to have no hesitation in asking again if we need to. I smiled at them and made sure to emphasise that we'd certainly come back to them, because we really were in dire need. His parents were a little taken aback at my reply. They gave an awkward laugh, but still encouraged me to do so. And Ruedi glared at me as if I'd made a gaffe in public. I'll definitely pay you back, for sure, he'd promised.

In the kitchen this morning, Ruedi seems afraid. He's afraid for himself, for us. He's afraid of what might happen to us. Of what's already happening to us. This is no time to hassle him as I've got into the habit of doing since I stopped working for Nkamba African Beauty. I repeat that if he doesn't want to ask for his parents' help, then he'll have to work. Find a little job. A student job, for instance. Waiter in a bar or restaurant. Call-centre operator. School supervisor. That's definitely possible.

He always replies by nodding. As if to stop me going on at him, he half-heartedly says yes. Yes, he'll do it. Yes, he's already looking. Then nothing. There's no hint that he's looking for anything at all. When he's not at the university, he spends his days in front of his computer.

For a while he's shut me up with his killer argument. He reminds me that it's hard to find work. You should understand that better than anyone, he says. Of course I understand. I have no choice. When I point out that even so he could make a bit more of an effort, he blames the French cross-border workers. They're the ones who are stealing our jobs, those Frouzes. He speaks without much conviction. But he says it all the same. Besides, he's far from being the only person I know to make that accusation. Monsieur Nkamba said so too. He'd drone on about it all day long, with such palpable anger that I wondered whether he'd eventually want a wall to be built to separate the true Eidgenossen like him from those parasitic foreigners. There are so many people around me muttering or shouting about it that, even if I keep quiet, I can't help asking myself: supposing they're right?

Ruedi takes all the yellow coins. He counts them again to make sure I haven't made a mistake. He confirms the total: eleven francs thirty-five.

I suggest a fifty-fifty split. Ruedi says no. That won't even buy me a packet of cigarettes, he argues. So what do we do with it, I quiz him with my eyes. He sighs and looks at the floor. A few seconds, then he gives in. In a semblance of a consensus, we decide that I will inherit the entire pile of gombo. I can do what I like with it. I consider the sacrifice that Ruedi has just made. I promise myself not to let him down. Then I tell myself it's his fault if we're in this predicament. He should just accept gombo from his parents. He still refuses.

No. He only refuses when I will also benefit from it . . .

I opt to buy a phone card to call my mother back in Bantuland. I go to one of the neighbourhood 24/7 shops: 'LycaMobile or Lebara?' 'Lebara.' 'Ten francs please.' Then, with the remaining one franc thirty-five, I buy some treats to sweeten the taste in my jaded mouth. Bitter.

Once home, I phone my mother. I'm not too sure what to say to her. I'm certainly not going to ask her to send me a little gombo from over there. That would be shameful. Nor am I going to tell her that my boyfriend and I are only going to get through the coming days thanks to the provisions she sent from Bantuland. That would be the ultimate humiliation! Nor will I tell her that I've just blown our entire fortune simply to hear the sound of her voice.

I'm going to have to lie. That will be best for everyone.

I'm going to tell her that everything is fine here. That I'm happy. Very happy, even. I'm going to make up the most outrageous stuff: that soon I'll be sending her some shiny gombo, loads of it. That I've just found a very well-paid job in a major international corporation based in Geneva. That soon I'm going to buy myself a very big villa on the shores of Lake Geneva, or a mountain chalet in Davos. That I'll visit her in Bantuland every month and even every weekend if she likes. I'll even tell her that my companion is a few weeks' overdue and that soon he'll be giving birth to a beautiful baby. That she'll have the honour of rocking this first ever child born of two biological fathers. That she'll be able to take it to school, cook it a dish of cassava with a palm-oil-based sauce, sing it Bantu lullabies and tell it tales from the Grison Alps, which she's never seen.

'I'm starting a little work placement in a few days' time,' I end up mumbling into the telephone.

'Oh Nzambe! You haven't mentioned this before. You always play hide-and-seek with your mother.' Mama speaks in a hoarse voice.

'Forget it. I'm not playing hide-and-seek. It's just a little three-month thing.'

'In any case, praise be to Nzambe! You must be pleased. You see, patience pays off. You just have to pray. Nzambe, Elolombi and the Bankoko always help their poor little children.'

'Let it be so.'

My mother rabbits on about Nzambe, God the father. About Elolombi, god of the spirits that hover over our souls, between heaven and earth. And the Bankoko, our ancestors who watch over our lives and grant our most heartfelt desires. 'Let it be so,' and 'Amen to that,' I keep replying automatically.

'After this work placement, Nzambe will help you find a real-real well-paid job,' she says.

'Uh-huh.'

'We say amen,' she corrects me.

'Amen.'

I have been taken on as an intern in a small NGO that campaigns against racial discrimination – whoops! Discrimination based on ethnicity – and the promotion of diversity. I think they took me on because I tick all their boxes, including . . . race. But what does it matter, says my mother on the phone, the main thing is that you got the job. Anyway, she concludes, the goat eats the grass where it is tethered.

What will I be doing in this association? I'll be writing letters of all kinds for the NGO's regular and potential partners. I will be writing and printing them out, and putting them on the desk of the director, Madame Bauer, whose eyes have deteriorated with age and the numerous angry battles she's waged. Madame Bauer can no longer cope with reading on any kind of screen. Even less on computer screens. It's all for young people, all these devices we have today, she tells me at our first meeting. With her gnarled hands, she then takes from her handbag her latest technological novelty: a hand-held magnifying glass.

The daughter of a Zurich banker, Madame Bauer grew up in the very swanky Goldküste – the so-called Swiss Gold Coast on the shores of Lake Zurich. She always says that it was in Geneva that she found her freedom to live, but in particular the freedom to fight. 'Fight' is a word that is often heard from the lips of Madame Bauer, a delightful old woman who behaves like a rebel. It is perhaps the sole character trait that time hasn't withered.

A rebel. Madame Bauer the rebel. She always wears lots of different colours, but especially green, in every shade: the archetypal eco-warrior. Which of course she is. She proclaims her veganism loud and clear. Not because it's trendy, she insists at every opportunity, but out of conviction for over forty years. Well before Brigitte Bardot, she concludes.

But, beneath her outer shell, I can easily read between her wrinkles and her rebel persona concealing her sensitivity that deep down there's a certain residue of privilege which she'd dearly love to shed. Apart from this eco-boho side, she has other strong traits. For example, when I first met her, the thing that struck me most was her husky voice. A voice that is too gravelly for her stature. Such a tiny woman, but with a very virile voice. Maybe it's the effect of her smoking and drinking. That's what she lives on. Dope, too.

Talking to my mother on the phone that evening, I hear something worrying in her voice. It sounds even huskier than that of my future internship boss. My mother doesn't usually sound that hoarse. Quite the opposite; she has a smooth, sing-song voice. I dismiss my anxiety and naively put this changed voice down to her excitement at my latest news.

'What about you, how are you?' I ask.

'Oh, I'm fine. Just a little sore throat that's making my head hot.'

'I thought so.'

'But nothing serious. Just a little sore throat, you know. When it's had enough of bothering me, it will go on its way. Nothing to worry about.'

Among our people, over there in Bantuland, it's not good – not at all good! – to have a sore throat, or worse, to be so ill that you lose your voice. It's a very bad sign. It means that the gods are no longer with you. Could our gods have abandoned Monga Minga? Could Nzambe have withdrawn to his heavens up there, leaving Monga Minga in the hands of evil spirits? Doesn't Elolombi, the god who protects our souls, recognise my mother's soul any more? And what about the Bankoko, our ancestors, are so they displeased with Monga Minga that they have to snatch her breath, her voice? Are they so angry at her that they are allowing a spirit of darkness to make her swallow germs while she's asleep?

I can sense that this sore throat is consuming my mother.

She's ashamed of it.

'Have you seen a doctor?'

'Drop this matter. I told you it's just a little sore throat, it's nothing, and it will clear up by itself.'

'The woman who conceals her pregnancy dies because of the child.'

'Who says I'm ashamed?'

'You must go and see a doctor.'

'Oh, but I already have!'

'And? So what do they say?'

'You know the doctas in our country! A bunch of incompetents!'

She tells me she's seen several doctas. All that for nothing. The doctas of Bantuland know nothing about the real-real medicine of the Whites, she claims. Some of them diagnosed bronchitis or pharyngitis or even a simple throat infection. Others spoke of a shrinking of the oesophagus. She continues, telling me that recently she went to a private hospital for the wealthy, and there they told her that it was probably a tumour in the throat. What nonsense! She takes offence. Tumour? Cancer? she queries in her phlegmy voice. Then she blurts out: but that's a disease of the rich! That's a White person's disease. How can a poor Bantu like me suffer from cancer?

Monga Minga carries on talking. She is pretty angry at the Bantu health system that diagnoses cancer – the ultimate disease of the rich – in the poor little patients of Bantuland. Is that responsible? she asks me. It's witchcraft! she exclaims. That's the only word those doctas have in their mouths these days: cancer. If it's not cancer, it's AIDS. Cancer or AIDS. That's what they tell you even when you've certainly got just a touch of malaria. They should leave the Whites' medicine to the Whites and go back to our country's traditional medicine.

My mother complains. Again and again. She says she's already bought lots of medication. For nothing. She seems disillusioned. She says that these drugs made her feel better for one day, and then the next day she felt even worse. Who could you trust? They all tell you the first thing that comes into their heads and pocket their share of gombo for doing nothing. Those doctas are thieves! she yells at me down the phone: they're all thieves! I hold the receiver away from my ear but continue to listen to her anguish.

'And now, how do you feel now?' I ask.

'I'm happy for you, my Mwana. This work placement of yours will open doors for you.'

'No,' I say, 'your throat?'

'It's still a bit sore, but Nzambe hears our prayers. He will crush our enemies' wickedness.'

A fireworks display has just begun in the harbour. The noise can be heard as far as our apartment and disrupts my conversation with Monga Minga. Besides, I have to ring off if I want to use my phone card again.

After I end the call, a series of images scrolls through my mind. I see my mother in a rusty, rickety bed back home in a hospital in Bantuland, suffocating due to a shrinking oesophagus. *Cioè*, I see her with twenty or so other patients in a hospice ward, each one facing death. I see her wasting away slowly-slowly without my being able to be at her side to give her a proper little kiss and cuddle. I picture her lying there on a thin mattress, all shrivelled, her skin pale, very pale even, her eyes bulging and wandering, her body frail and thin. These images make me very upset . . .

Ruedi is standing behind me. He places a hand on my shoulder. He's probably heard most of my conversation with Monga Minga. I tell him that she's sick. She must be very sick, I say. But it's not serious, I add. Well, actually, we don't know whether it's serious or not.

Ruedi puts his arms around me. A loud firework explosion goes off outside. The smell of sulphur assails my nostrils. I sneeze.

While Ruedi strokes my back, I try to swallow my saliva. I try to do this to imagine the suffering torpedoing my mother. It must be here, or here, or even here. The throat seems to be quite long. The oesophagus? What exactly is that? And where is it precisely? Is it here, or here? I only know that it's somewhere in the throat. Perhaps around the Adam's apple? But no, in Bantuland they say that women don't have this Adam's apple. My mother might have an Eve's cassava, but definitely not an Adam's apple.

Well, she could come here for treatment, suggests Ruedi, suddenly inspired. I gaze at him for a long time, then I reply: I've just bought a Lebara phone card with all the money we had left.

5

The thing that hits you immediately in this waiting room is, is . . . how can I put it . . . ? I'd say: the silence. The kind of silence that conveys neither mourning, nor hunger, nor even need. All seems well. You might even wonder what on earth people are doing here. Do they come to read the freebie newspapers that mockingly inform them that the number of unemployed is continually falling, whereas they still can't land anything at all, not even a bullshit job? Do they come to read magazines full of Gucci-Dior-Chanel ads for products they'll never buy, not even in their dreams? Do they come to check out the few job ads on the walls which they've seen and seen again a thousand times elsewhere and especially online? Or do they simply come back to see the fixed artificial smile of an adviser paid to remind them, with a snooty look, that they're not doing enough to help themselves?

Silence. Impatience. There's a really weird guy over there, right next to the door that leads to the advisers' offices. Maybe it'll be his turn soon. He's in a big-big hurry. He looks embarrassed. Anxious. He doesn't want to be there one moment longer. He looks about him as if he is afraid someone will recognise him. I guess he's ashamed. I want to tell him not to worry, that we're all up shit creek. But is that what I'm here for? I let him be.

Silence. Impatience. The distance too. A spotty youth has massive headphones clamped over his ears. He's nodding his head. It must be rap. I wonder what the hell he's doing here. At that age, kids are still in nappies. But am I here for him? I let him be. Next to him, a dark-haired woman with a red fur coat seems to be very busy staring at something on the screen of her Clamshell iBook. I so want to ask her if she belongs to the class of nouveau poor who cling to the last vestiges of a glorious past life. But is that what I'm here for? I let her be too. A few feet from her, there's a man with a stubbly chin and completely white hair, with a defeated look. Even so, he's suited and booted and wearing a tie. Probably the remnants of a past era, like the lady and the iBook with its hand grip. He must be in his early sixties. His brooding gaze is riveted on a corner of the carpeted floor of the waiting room. What's he staring at over there? I'll never know. He's elsewhere. Far away. Too far away in his thoughts. He doesn't bat an eyelid even at the sound of a phone ringing in the room. He barely even notices the constant gesticulations of the anxious guy who hastily disappears when his adviser comes to fetch him. From his face, I can gauge the depth of his despair. His story is perhaps that of an entrepreneur who's come a cropper, and is up to his neck in the mire. Perhaps it's also that of a family man, overwhelmed by fate. I have no idea. All I can do for him is let him be.

This entire atmosphere suddenly irritates my throat. I cough noisily. A few pairs of eyes stare at me. Embarrassment has me doubled over. My armpits begin to drip sweat. To distance myself from all those eyes roving over me, I think of my mother. I wonder how she's feeling this morning. I'd like to know whether our phone conversation yesterday helped soothe her sore throat a little, or whether that voice that's even huskier than Madame Bauer's is still lurking in her throat. I cough again. I fear a shrinking of my oesophagus. What am I saying? I'm being stupid.

I don't have the time to think too much about my throat or my mother's because a man comes out of my adviser's office. It's the third office down the corridor on the left. You can see it from the waiting room. The man is out of his mind with fury. He's so enraged that he's like a madman. He slams my adviser's door behind him with a loud bang. Everyone jumps. The guy with the stubble jumps too. At last! The pimply youth removes his headphones from his rabbit ears. The lady with the iBook with a hand grip looks up from her device. That's the end of the silence-impatience-distance mode we shared until then. The room begins to buzz like a beehive. The furious guy bangs his fists on the walls, then on the doors. *Fuck you! Fuck off!* he yells. Fuck this fucking shitty system! Shit! Fucking shit! The buzzing spreads through the room like an epidemic. People pretend to whisper into their neighbour's ear, when in fact, they're talking to themselves. He's right, after all. *Fuck!* I could read on the lips of the iBook lady. Her face is so painted that if it were up to me, boss, I'd never have hired her in my business. But even so, he's overreacting, says an indignant man who looks like a hated concierge. His file will be closed. For sure! concludes his neighbour. We all agree: his case is nasty! Gazes wander, meet, brush against each other, apologise, then light in unison upon the deviant. The black sheep. Who, through his behaviour, seems to provide a reason for the presence of all of us here.

Our eyes follow the pissed-off guy as he storms out of the room into the main corridor. In the lift, the nutter smashes his fist into the mirror. *Fuck!* The noise. He's shattered the glass. Shock. We're all on our feet. Panic. The security guards arrive. What we're seeing here is just a taster!

I'd always wondered why they'd put that fucking mirror in the lift. Look at yourself. Yes, you! I'm talking to you. Go on, look at yourself in the mirror. Can you see yourself? Can you see what a loser you are? A loser! You're just a good-for-nothing. Do you really think you'll be able to get through this? No way!

OK! If you say so. We'll soon see! Come on, get out of here fast, poor idiot! Piss off! Go on, fuck off! Poor loser. You're a loser! A loser! Those words rang in my ears each time I came out of the lift. You're a loser! I think the nutter received those same insults from that mirror too, and that he didn't exactly appreciate the insolent tone. So, he smashed it.

Shortly afterwards, my adviser herself arrived, erect in her little heels, her smile carefully confined to the corners of her mouth. Her mask was back in place. She came over to me and held out a stiff hand. As usual.

My adviser is a lady who's knee-high to a frog. She's got an excess of marge in her body, as you can see from her pudgy face and her triple chin. She's probably got it around her hips and her rear end. Three blond hairs play hopscotch on her head. I often wonder why she doesn't give herself a good old kongolibon like me. A shaven head would definitely suit her better than those three hairs she insists on nurturing.

Despite the mask, you can clearly see the traces of what she has just endured. She is full of shame. Shame to end all shame. Of fear too. She's rigid. Glacial.

In her office, she takes her seat at her computer and has a sip of water. She flicks through my file, folds her hands on her desk and looks at me.

'Go ahead. I'm listening,' she says.

'I wanted to tell you that I've found an internship.'

'Really? Well done!'

It's weird: I'm happy to see that my news seems to reinvigorate the lady.

'Is it paid? Full-time?' she asks.

I tell her it is. I tell her how I managed to get this work placement. It's a friend of a friend of the boyfriend of a colleague of my sister Kosambela who recommended this organisation. Great networking opportunity, she says. It's about having contacts, I retort. She doesn't allow this attack to rile her. She's already fought a hard battle. She'd rather display her joy for me.

'What happens to my file now?' I ask.

'We're going to close it.'

'So, good for the statistics.'

'You mustn't see things that way, Monsieur Mwana. If you have found a full-time paid internship, I don't see why we should keep your file open.'

'But it's only for three months.'

'In the meantime, we'll close it anyway.'

'I haven't had any support from you.'

'Please,' she protests with a hint of annoyance, 'don't start that again.'

Now she's being herself. The mask drops.

'On the other hand, I advise you to carry on looking for work,' she concludes.

That night, on the phone, I report the events to my mother whose voice is still as hoarse as the day before. I'm highly selective about what I tell her. The spat between my adviser and the angry guy is ideal. Surely Nzambe couldn't stand by and allow that woman to destroy people like that, says my mother. You can't imagine how I laughed, I lie. We laugh. We forget our problems for the time being. Then Monga Minga puts a damper on things. She says that she finds that I complain a bit too much. A lot too much. That perhaps I'm a bit pessimistic. That I must stay hopeful. That I must carry on looking. And, she adds, the hen that seeks never goes to bed hungry. That's right, it's the true-truth, I answer.

My mother carries on giving me advice. She reminds me that being unemployed for a few months, even unpaid, isn't the end of the world. In Bantuland, she adds, public servants sometimes go months without being paid. How do they live? They live like the birds in the sky: they neither sow nor harvest, they store nothing in the granaries . . . and besides, my mother goes on, haven't you just found a work placement? So why complain?

While Monga Minga speaks, I'm more concerned by her rasping voice than by what she's saying.

6

It isn't Mireille Laudenbacher, Madame Bauer's secretary and dogsbody, who comes and opens the door to me this morning. She's embroiled again in a whole load of red tape to save her dog from being put down. Meanwhile, the situation here is serious, Madame Bauer tells me, stubbing out the cigarette whose last fumes she's just puffed out.

I find Madame Bauer very elegant. A floral turquoise dress brushes against her calves revealing her cherry-pink tights. A pair of vintage brown kitten heels makes her look like a tap dancer, and a jacket of recycled woollens is draped over her shoulders. She's wearing a red wool felt hat that has an oval flower brooch pinned to the side.

She lets me take my place in the same chair I sat in the first time I met her. With an exaggeratedly nonchalant gesture, she pours herself a cup of green tea and raises it gingerly to her lips. She leaves a red lipstick mark. She lights another cigarette. Oh, excuse me, Mwana – she uses my first name – do you want a coffee? A tea?

I shake my head. She smiles at me fondly and adjusts her hat. She sits down facing me.

A telephone rings. It's the one on Mireille Laudenbacher's desk, across the room. As nimble as a young woman, Madame Bauer rolls her chair backwards and picks up the phone. Ah, my dear friend Khalifa! she exclaims theatrically. While she chats to her dear friend Khalifa, I get up and take a tour of the room. I spot a poster for the *Ni putes ni soumises* movement. A poster featuring a little girl with a determined face; at the bottom are the words 'When a little girl grows up, she becomes a woman. Not a whore or a doormat'. Or both, I think with a smile. I stealthily continue my inspection. I see so many posters. There's one that says: 'No to racism'. Another calls for rich countries to contribute 0.7% of their GDP to development aid for the global South. A poster in the corner reads 'End domestic violence'. Another shows two visibly happy women with their little boy. All these posters are vying with each other in originality. But there is one poster on the other side of the room, just behind Madame Bauer, that particularly catches my attention. It shows rainbow-coloured sheep chasing a sheep from the National Liberation Movement (NLM) against a backdrop of the Swiss flag – a red background with a white cross. It has the slogan: 'We're not sheep'. I smile all the more. It's a parody of the black sheep that I saw for the first time in July in Lugano.

I go back to my seat at Madame Bauer's desk. A pile of stray papers has set up home there. Just next to all the bumph is a big ashtray that must rarely sit idle. Madame Bauer bellows so loudly into the phone that it sounds as if she's having an argument with her dear friend Khalifa. She seems angry. Or rather . . . appalled. She soon ends her noisy conversation peppered with 'it's scandalous!', and 'it's unacceptable!'. 'Mwana,' she says, hanging up.

'Yes?'

'I've written a press release. Can you send it to this list of contacts?'

'Where's the press release?'

'Just there on my desk.'

It's a handwritten press release. It peels away easily from the pile of papers in front of me. While I familiarise myself with the document that I'll have to type up on a computer before emailing it to a flock of journalists, Madame Bauer talks non-stop. She keeps repeating 'it's scandalous' and 'it's unacceptable!' It's scandalous, such poster campaigns, she says. All that for the sole purpose of winning votes. It's populism! It's dishonest! She's outraged. But we're not going to sit here and do nothing, she warns. While she talks, I read the press release entitled: 'Rainbow sheep: stop xenophobia!' I then realise that Madame Bauer and her dear friend Khalifa and plenty of others too are planning a march on Lausanne, on 18 September, to demonstrate their anger at the black-sheep poster.

'What do you think, Mwana?' Madame Bauer asks.

I'm surprised at her question.

'It's appalling,' I say.

'That's racism, isn't it?'

'Absolutely.'

Faced with my laconic replies, my internship supervisor decides to briefly change the subject. She explains how her association works. They do this, they do that. In normal times, they only operate at fifty per cent capacity at the most. They don't have the resources to be active full-time. And she had to admit that age was beginning to play mean tricks on her. She doesn't have the stamina to fight as she used to. But now, with this black sheep poster, the situation is serious. That's why she's thinking of working full-time at least until the federal elections. A few generous friends have supported her financially. She tells me she's working flat out to see this struggle through to the end. That the younger generation is less politically engaged than her generation.

I've done some things in my lifetime, she states with a smile full of nostalgia. She tells me that she took part in the first environmental and anti-nuclear campaigns, and those against men's other idiocies. Those men even thought themselves so clever, so brilliant, that they didn't want to grant her the right to vote – her, a woman. All women. And *they* called their vote universal suffrage? she asked sarcastically. She fought like a madwoman against the Vietnam war, against the occupation of the countries of Africa, against the Schwarzenbach Initiative in 1970 to limit immigration into Switzerland, against the apartheid regime in South Africa. She pauses. The Schwarzenbach Initiative! she exclaims, and her raspy voice goes right through me. She seems to be getting carried away. Then she calms down. A silence that speaks volumes. I don't know what to say. She helps herself to another cigarette, then blurts out: sadly nothing has really changed!

At midday, Madame Bauer is going to have lunch with her dear friend Khalifa. She promises she'll introduce him to me one day. He's a really good man, she says.

I don't fancy wandering around the city during my break. That would be to waste my energy for nothing. It would only intensify my hunger. So I stay in the office. I'm bored. At one point, I phone my sister Kosambela. I want to tell her about my first day as an intern. She doesn't let me get two sentences out. She tells me she hasn't got time, she's not on her break yet. But she does quickly mutter one piece of news: she tells me that there might be a way to bring Monga Minga over here to Switzerland for treatment. What?! I ask in disbelief. She hangs up.

Madame Bauer spends the afternoon between the phone and paperwork. She's fine-tuning the organisation of her demonstration. As for me, I continue to acquaint myself with the association's main activities and the issues it's dealing with. My nose in numerous documents, I understand the reasons behind the poster they're protesting against. The NLM wants to send all the foreign criminals back to their home countries – the infamous black sheep. I surf the website of Madame Bauer's NGO. Naturally, it has one. It reflects the organisation's limited financial means. It must be the work of Mireille Laudenbacher, herself a woman from another generation that has little experience of computer technology. I read the many press releases written by my supervisor. The tone is the same: highly politicised, trenchant, accusatory and even peremptory. Madame Bauer, in the name of her association and of her long experience as a human-rights activist, has a position on various issues ranging from combating racism to the struggle for gender equality. There are also the questions of homophobia, North–South relations, abortion or the condition of single mothers, and so on. She's got a finger in every pie.

It will soon be four o'clock. Madame Bauer tells me I can go home if I like. She says I must feel free. We're free here, she adds, swivelling on her chair. The main thing is that the work gets done.

When I arrive home, I tell Ruedi about my first day at work. I tell him it's brilliant. That Madame Bauer is an amazing woman, committed, tough, despite her advanced age. I tell him about the demo she's organising in Lausanne on 18 September.

'Great!' he agrees. 'She sounds cool.'

'That's all she's done her entire life: fight. She must enjoy it. Today she had me send her press release to loads and loads of journalists.'

'She means business, then.'

'No kidding,' I retort, removing my shoes. 'I just hope that she'll be able to keep a lid on her anger until the day of the demo.'

Ruedi says we need people like Madame Bauer to change the mindset in this country. I remind him that he's against the cross-border workers.

'Stealing other people's jobs is a crime,' he says.

'So should we send them back to France, then?'

'I don't know. The people will decide.'

Ruedi falls silent then. He's never really been convinced by this argument even though he keeps repeating it.

I'm lying on the bed. My belly starts rumbling. I ask Ruedi if there's maybe a little something to eat.

'There are still some bobolos in the freezer,' he teases.

'Are the potatoes you brought back from your parents already finished?'

'What potatoes?' he asks, laughing. 'Don't you like the food from Bantuland any more?'

'Ruedi, don't wind me up.'

Ruedi serves me a few boiled potatoes with a plain tomato sauce. I devour the whole thing like a starveling. I drink a lot of water. That's the secret. Drink a lot of water to fill the hollow.

7

The Manager-Sisters agreed to care for Monga Minga at their private hospital, San Salvatore. They pulled out all the stops to get her out of Bantuland. They accepted her in their establishment, out of charity, with no guarantee of payment. Well, almost. Because even charity has its limits. You can't have your coconut cake and eat it . . .

The Manager-Sisters performed this generous act for the glory of God. They have always maintained that their work is not only that of making money, but also, and most importantly, to please God through charitable works. But the Manager-Sisters also acted thus in response to a specific request from their protégée in Christ, Kosambela.

My sister, Kosambela, works as a cleaner in the San Salvatore hospital in Lugano. It's a private hospital perched on the hills above the town. From there, you can see the sun's rays reflected in the tranquil waters of Lake Lugano. Alongside the hospital patients sits the splendid bell tower of the very ancient church of San Salvatore, whose chimes ring out through the cool air and remind each person of God's omnipresence. Kosambela claims that it's no coincidence that the Manager-Sisters of the past chose to build a bell tower in that spot. She says that it's there, right next to the San Salvatore hospital, to drive out all the evil spirits prowling around the patients. She also says that in that place there must be ongoing battles between the forces of evil and the forces of good. When she rabbits on about that, I yawn.

Every time I've visited my sister at her workplace, I've been struck by the number of crucifixes and other religious symbols in the waiting rooms, corridors, lifts, wards and even in the toilets. Anyone would think that the good lord – Nzambe, as my mother in Bantuland would call him – has become a sort of Big Brother who follows us everywhere.

Like any self-respecting cleaner, Kosambela is very often tired and on sick leave. All that because of the backache that dogs her despite her young age. But little do her backache and her frequent days off sick matter to the Manager-Sisters at the San Salvatore hospital, who are very fond of her. Seeing the privileges they grant her, it seems as if they they're prepared to give whatever it takes to keep her in their employment. As if Kosambela had even become a sort of saint.

Kosambela never indulges in blasphemy or other swear words – even though they are commonplace in the language of Dante. If you say to her *Porca puttana di merda*, she replies: may God bless you. If you add *Cazzo di merda*, she replies: may God bless you. And even if you say *Porco Dio!* she still replies . . . may God bless you. When you ask how she is, she replies: well, by the grace of God. And if anyone mentions her backache, she replies, rolling her eyes heavenwards: it will pass, by the grace of God. Only the name of her ex-husband can dent her pious air by a fraction. When you ask her, how's Antonio, she answers: Who? That thing? Then she adds, adjusting her headscarf: God alone knows.

Just before the end of visiting hour, at around 8 p.m., the PA system unleashes a long prayer throughout the hospital – in the corridors, in the wards, in the canteen, in the cloakrooms and even in the loos. It is the mission of the Manager-Sisters. Holy Mary mother of God, pray for us poor sinners! Our Father who art in heaven, hallowed be Thy name! . . . Amen. And while the Sisters pray, Kosambela wrecks her knees, just next door, in the Church of San Salvatore. She does that every night before going home. And that's how she managed to earn the respect of the Manager-Sisters who must sometimes see in her the Holy Ghost dancing to the rhythm of the balafons from back in our country.

Kosambela likes to suss people out before talking to them, because she's one of those people who know that a bird doesn't settle on an unknown tree. And it can be said that Pierpaolo Bernasconi was not such an unknown branch for her. She loved this oncologist from the hospital very much. She had introduced him to me one day. We were in a supermarket. He's a slim man with a well-groomed appearance, educated and very elegant. He's a really good person, this guy, my sister had told me. A good person, you can sense it straightaway! No need to complicate things, it's obvious, she was forever telling me.

When she spoke of Bernasconi, it wasn't only to tell me how wonderful she thought he was. She sang his praises constantly and held him up as a role model for me to follow. You've got to get out of your village ways, *fratellino*, she went on at me non-stop. Look at Signore Bernasconi! He's handsome and clever. He knows how to talk to women, even a lowly cleaning woman like me. I want you to be like him. You'll be the pride of our family and the whole of Bantuland. Oh, Signore Bernasconi!

I think that no one had been happier than Kosambela to learn that Doctor Bernasconi was getting married. Finally! exclaimed my sister, then added that Nzambe had heard her prayers. Because she had always prayed for him. She was convinced that all he needed was a wife, a proper spouse, children, a family and the whole shebang that goes with it. God doesn't sleep! she'd said.

My sister didn't need asking twice to go Doctor Bernasconi's engagement party. She'd invited me to go with her because she wanted to share that happy moment with me. You have to see how God blesses those who walk in His ways.

I've rarely seen Kosambela display such genuine, intense and . . . palpable joy. Since her thing of a husband left, she smiles less and less, and her hyperactive sons and constant backache don't make her life any easier. But now I was seeing a different Kosambela. The one I'd lost the habit of seeing.

In general, when my sister goes to parties given by people from Bantuland, she stays in a corner, not reacting or budging. While her fellow partygoers buzz around each other and sway to the electric beat of the kalimbas or balafons, she remains seated. Calm. She maintains that she doesn't want to get caught up in all those banalities. The children of God don't do those things. They are earthly pleasures, of the flesh. Whereas now, all she wants are spiritual pleasures. And the only thing that can still give her the spiritual pleasures she so craves is food! During the Bantu festivals organised in Switzerland, no question she would ever miss the opportunity to stuff herself with fresh-fresh ndoleh straight from Bantuland: saka-saka, fumbua, smoked bush meat, fried ripe plantains or bobolos.

And yet, at that engagement party in a karaoke pub in Bellinzona, Kosambela had let her hair down. She had even gone so far as to drink wine. Oh Nzambe! She'd danced, danced, danced. She'd shimmied and shaken her hips. She'd sung in Bernasconi's honour: *Tu mi fai girar, tu mi fai girar, come fossi una bambola.* She sang out of tune. No one cared. Seeing Kosambela sing what she had always considered to be banalities, that was simply unheard-of.

At the end of the party, Kosambela had given me a lift, along with one of her colleagues, the one whose friend of a friend of her boyfriend had suggested I contact Madame Bauer.

'You sing really well,' her colleague commented.

'*Grazie,*' Kosambela replied, chuffed.

'The Sisters from the hospital should have seen you,' teased the colleague.

Kosambela didn't reply straightaway. That remark had doubtless made her realise later that she'd gone a little bit too far. But what wouldn't she have done for Doctor Bernasconi?

'And now you mention them,' Kosambela went on, 'why didn't the Sisters from the hospital come to the party? Their presence would have made Paolo Bernasconi even happier.'

'What?!? Haven't you heard the latest?!'

'What? Tell me.'

'The Sisters boycotted Bernasconi's party because he's marrying a man in Spain.'

'Aieee, Nzambe!' My sister slammed on the brakes, in the middle of the motorway.

A car ran into the back of us . . .

We were all safe and sound. Kosambela took two weeks' sick leave. This time it wasn't for her backache, but to pray to Nzambe and the angels to forgive her for going to the engagement party of that kind of man. A sinner! The Manager-Sisters understood and forgave her. Amen.

8

The controversial poster has all tongues wagging. There are opinions of every flavour. Some say there's nothing nasty about it. It's just an everyday expression, they argue. A black sheep is simply someone who's a bit different from its fellow sheep. Nothing more. Others, however, claim that it contains blatant discrimination against foreigners.

On this subject, anything is permitted. People kick the topic about. They tackle. They hurl insults. They slap one another down through interviews and posters.

Yesterday I went to Caritas to tell them I was hungry. For sure they gave me a coupon for the food bank. But they still added that my situation was made worse by the poster . . . Here we go again! On the train to work this morning, two young passengers, clearly friends, almost came to blows arguing about it . . . Upset, I changed compartments. I just needed a little break. A little moment to myself when I didn't have to think, or speak or hear about this issue. In another compartment, I found some peace next to an elderly lady who was with a girl who must have been her granddaughter. The elderly lady immediately smiled at me. That soothed me. Then she carried on smiling at me and staring at me for the entire remainder of the journey. Weird. Why was she smiling at me so much? I wondered. Then she said, 'You know I'm not one of those people who think you're a black sheep, I'm not!'

In the end, I had to stand by a door waiting just to get out. Get out of this world where a poster can stir up so much feeling. But for how long?

It's the day of the big demo against the poster of discord. At the office, we're all prepared to go out into the streets this afternoon: banners, placards, whistles, megaphones, and above all a large dose of indignation and anger. We make the effort to learn the slogans by heart: 'No to xe-no-phobia!', 'Down with racism!'

Mireille Laudenbacher is here today. More energetic than ever. There's a chance that her dog will be spared the lethal injection. That gives her the courage and the strength she needs to take on this other fight. She goes to and fro. The clattering of her heels makes an unbearable sound. A sound that thumps me in the belly and stirs up my hunger. There's a lot to do, but she won't delegate anything. These are things that require experience, she replies kindly when I ask if I can give her a hand.

There's a journalist standing in our open-plan office. He writes for a local paper, Mireille Laudenbacher whispers as she is coming and going. The guy has chubby cheeks and looks good-natured. One hand is pressing against the base of his spine and his shoulders are pulled back: this posture must be essential to support his heavy belly. I invite him to have a seat. He thanks me and sits down gingerly on a small chair which I'm now worried will collapse with a horrible crash. He tells me he's here to interview Madame Bauer. I hope she'll be free soon, he says. Madame Bauer is across the office. She's being photographed, smiling, in front of the poster showing rainbow sheep and the sign saying: 'We're not sheep'. She's all fired up. She'll be even more excited when another journalist, this time from a more important daily paper, turns up. It must be hard being so much in demand, but most of all it's such a thrill. You can see it in Madame Bauer's eyes. She's like a kid meeting Father Christmas.

But, to be honest, this hasn't always been the case. In the early days, Madame Bauer didn't have the opportunity to give interviews. She herself told me so. In the early days, no one took her in the least bit seriously. No one took any interest in her when, nearly forty years ago, she launched her first battles against nuclear power stations or the discharge of aluminium waste into the Rhône. People thought she was a nutter, bonkers.

They must even have thought her bitter and twisted when she demanded the vote for women in the whole of Switzerland. But all those marks of disrespect are now behind her. She has proved herself, even though she has rarely won her battles. And now, suddenly, everything has changed. Madame Bauer has gained recognition, not only from her fellow campaigners but also from politicians, the press and everyone who likes to express their opinion. And now, when there's an issue around one of her pet causes, countless journalists come and thrust their microphone in front of her to gather her opinion. They want the view of the expert. Expert Bauer. Her opinion has become a crucial seasoning to enhance the taste of their articles and reportages.

During all the interviews she gives, I can see that Madame Bauer takes great pleasure in vehemently criticising the black-sheep poster. 'It's outrageous!' she exclaims between arguments punctuated with the recent history of humanity. She vaunts the values of solidarity, respect and humanism. When she evokes those values, the traits of my Bantuland people, I say to myself that she must be the most Bantu of all the Swiss.

My belly sings.

Madame Bauer gave me the job of revamping their website, even of designing a new one. I took this task seriously. Very, very seriously. Not only because it enabled me to score my first goals, but most importantly because it was a good way to distance myself from the subject that was on the tip of everyone's tongues. I didn't want my three-month internship to become a work placement campaigning against a poster. When I mulled over my thoughts, I realised that this poster had a nasty odour. But is it the smell of a poster that will put food on my plate? Will it even help cure my poor mother who's become the black sheep of the doctas in Bantuland?

I built a website which I update regularly. A website that only talks about the topic that's trending. Despite all my efforts to shake it off, this topic is everywhere around me. The latest news is all about this evening's demo.

Monsieur Khalifa, whom I finally met, said a big bravo! for my work. Monsieur Khalifa is a long, thin guy. He looks like a pencil. He's a Tunisian intellectual who has been settled here among our cousins for ages. He lives in the Vaud and his accent is even stronger than that of the natives of the deepest countryside. When he opens his mouth, it sounds as if it's Madame Bauer who's speaking. Same tone of voice, same indignation, but above all, same idea: 'it's outrageous!', 'it's unacceptable!'.

Today, while Mireille Laudenbacher is dealing with this sensitive matter, I spend my time reading the various online comments. On the whole, the people who visit my website are politically committed. They'll be at the demo later.

I'm hungry.

If my belly carries on singing like this, I'll enter a singing contest. It's days, weeks even, since I've been able to afford lunch. For dinner, I make do as best I can with a cassava bobolo, grilled peanuts, pundu, or boiled potatoes. Luckily there's a food bank distribution today. Ruedi will go and pick up our parcel.

Between responding to comments on my online forum, I write a job application. Of course I'm continuing to look for work, like the unemployment office lady said. Otherwise, in just over two months, at the end of my work placement, my belly will be singing even louder and I won't be able to offer it a solution.

I send out countless applications. The answer is always the same.

9

We're all assembled at Place de la Palud in Lausanne. The last wan rays of sunshine are gently fading. A gentle, cool wind caresses the faces pale with indignation that are beginning to darken Place de la Palud. The terrace of a bar across the square is still filled with customers clinging on to summer. A few onlookers gather in clusters. They stand a few metres away from us, but far enough so as to not to appear part of our movement. Some watch us, frowning, as if they are wondering what the hell we're doing there. Others, meanwhile, look at us and smile, as if they're about to applaud a carnival procession. The two expressions are not the same.

What's going on? I hear a young woman ask a man, who must be her partner. It's about the sheep, he replies. They both smile. The young woman fishes a little digital camera out of her pocket. She takes a few photos of the square, checks their quality, takes a few more, then they leave.

The march sets off in just under an hour. The troops are growing impatient and still need to be organised. They're raring to demonstrate. These uncommon occasions are not to be missed. Because it has to be said that demos are so unusual here in Switzerland that even the smallest one is a real occasion!

More and more people are congregating in the little Place de la Palud. There must be more than a thousand of us by now. The human mass is becoming harder and harder to contain. I'm not sure that Madame Bauer was expecting such a success. She must be smiling somewhere in front of the cameras and microphones of the journalists who've come to report on the event. Some hotheads begin to shout: 'Death to the party of hate!' A young woman who's clearly very angry had started off the chanting. She's standing on the Fontaine de la Justice. She can't help herself. No, she can't wait any longer. She yells again: 'Death to the party of hate!' A deafening booing ensues.

Oh, how infuriated Madame Bauer must be right now! That is absolutely not the slogan she'd envisaged for this demo. She waves Khalifa and Mireille Laudenbacher over and appeals to them. They simply have to get the demonstrators under control. Out of the question to see her plans go awry in front of all the media.

The human mass is becoming unmanageable. The owner of the bar across the square is starting to shut up shop. From his scared look, it's clear that he's afraid of how all this is going to end. He asks his customers lingering on the terrace to kindly make themselves scarce. The media rush over to the organisers to ask for their comments on this and that. Live, to boot! Madame Bauer's speeches are the absolute priority. She's the one that all the audiences must listen to at home as they're about to sit down for dinner. She has to tell them her truth about the black sheep issue.

While Madame Bauer is in ecstasy in front of the media who woo her, caress her and prod her, Monsieur Khalifa and other leaders of the demo are already in the procession. They're at its head. They need to get the impatient demonstrators moving. They're here to march, so let them march. They're here to bleat their anger loud and clear, so, let them bleat. That's how things have been organised: Monsieur Khalifa leads the flock, Mireille Laudenbacher plays the sheep dog and Madame Bauer presents the whole thing to the media.

My belly hasn't stopped singing all day.

I suddenly feel weak. I feel my strength ebbing. I won't have enough energy to get to the end of the demo. I stand to one side for a moment. I watch the crowd march past. I wonder what the hell I'm doing there. If I wasn't an intern in this NGO, would I have wanted to take part in this demo? And if I'd admitted to Madame Bauer that her demo didn't really interest me, what would she have done with me? After all, she is paying me for this internship, isn't she? I'm convinced that there may be something dodgy, even sickening about that poster of discord. But is that sufficient reason to ask myself to go on the demo with an empty belly?

I know that that poster can become even more insulting if you think for a moment about its sponsor. I heard via the media that it's a man who's rolling in gombo. He's got tonnes of it, they say. But they often say too that the sponsor of the poster of discord, head of the National Liberation Movement, doesn't like foreigners. Nkamba, my naturalised old boss, doesn't like them very much either. Since his naturalisation, he boasts of being an Eidgenosse, a true Swiss born and bred. He maintains point blank that priority should be given to Eidgenossen like him before thinking of others. I have every reason to believe that that's why he gave me the push. He needed a pure-blooded Swiss person to sell his fake goods. And had it not been for this summary dismissal, I wouldn't have ended up working for Madame Bauer, and I wouldn't be where I am right now, sitting on the pavement, my belly empty. I've read that the sponsor of the controversial poster wants to send the cross-border workers back to France. And me, I live with a delightful redhead who has no compunction about saying that the cross-border workers, from Savoie – the 'Frouzes' – are taking his potential jobs.

Ah, there's Mireille Laudenbacher. I get up and go over to meet her. Her hands are full of flags and placards, but above all she's holding a little see-through plastic bag in which I can see an apple and two chocolat croissants.

'Can I help you?'

'Yes, of course, Mwana. Hold this too. You can eat it.'

Never will Mireille Laudenbacher know how much good she did me that day in giving me an apple and two chocolate croissants.

The procession is heading to the other side of the city, towards the Tunnel. I peel away. I don't want to keep following it. First of all I have to calm the uprising in my gut. It's not the guy who's hungry who gets to eat, but the one who has food in his hand. And food I have. I sit on the steps overlooking the Rumine Palace on Place de la Riponne. I put the flags and placards that Mireille Laudenbacher had given me down on the ground. I bite into the Golden Delicious apple I'm holding. When I swallow the first piece, I feel my stomach churn like an earthworm that someone's thrown a few grains of salt onto. After the heaving, my stomach gradually calms down like a frenzied animal that has been tamed. The procession will just have to wait for me or ditch me. I'll join it later, once I've sorted out my gut problems. I take all the time in the world to eat my apple and my chocolate croissants. I'm in no hurry. When I finish eating, I go over to the fountain in the centre of the square where like a lamb I quench my thirst in the jet of pure water.

I lengthen my stride and manage to rejoin the procession. I'm perspiring like a street seller, especially as I'm carrying flags and placards. At Avenue de Vinet, a crowd of youths whistle. Great boos rise up like explosions. The demonstrators go wild. The youths run amok. They set dustbins on fire. I've never seen anything like that here. Back home, in Bantuland, it happens all the time and the perpetrators are crushed by the military who treat them like black sheep. But here, it's the first time I've seen this happening. I feel scared. Once again, I wonder what the hell I'm doing here. It's for my internship. It's for my pay cheque. It's for my belly. But now, the mercury's rising too high. It's not because you're hungry that you sell your teeth.

I decide to get away from there. I head south, towards the station. I go back to Geneva with a few flags and placards.

When I arrive home, I'm the happiest man in the world. An aroma of something very good makes me drool like a dog. Ruedi's cooked a lentil stew with vegetables and a few chunks of meat in it.

I stop in the kitchen, which is also our dining room and living room. I dump all the demo paraphernalia in a corner of the room. I pick up a plate and help myself to a portion that matches my belly's expectations. Ruedi sits down opposite me. He rests his elbows on the table. He places a hand on his cheek and watches me devour the stew. It takes me less than ten minutes to put the contents of my plate where it needs to be. I let out a big burp that makes my lips quiver. I scrape my plate with my spoon. Ruedi covers his ears with his hands – he can't bear the screeching sound. I help myself to seconds. He carries on gazing at me, amicably, affectionately. Lovingly?

'It's good, huh,' I say.

Ruedi smiles. He picks a placard up from the floor and reads aloud: 'We're not sheep!' He laughs and sits back down facing me. 'Lucky you're not a sheep,' he says.

I frown.

'You're already black.'

He's making fun of me. We laugh. A vegetable chunk falls off my over-heaped spoon and stains my shirt. Ruedi bursts out laughing.

'You eat like an animal.'

A jug of water is sitting right in front of me. 'You need to drink some water,' says Ruedi. I take a sip of water. I'm stuffed. One more spoonful and I'll puke.

I go into the bedroom. Slowly, I get undressed and lie down on our bed. Ruedi lies down beside me, his head under my armpit. He pulls away at once and makes a face.

'You need to take a shower.'

I leap up and grab him and wedge his head under my armpit. He groans. He struggles. I let him go. We laugh like kids. He commands me to go and have a shower. He says my armpits stink.

'Children and fools speak the truth,' I reply.

'Yeah, right! Go on, go and have a shower and stop being a smart-arse, he says, holding his nose.

I go into the bathroom. I wash my face in the washbasin. Ruedi stands in the doorway. I tell him all about the demo. I say there were a lot of people there. That some hooded youths smashed up everything. That they set everything on fire. That it was like in war films you often see on TV. Ruedi makes no comment. He knows I'm exaggerating.

I sit on the toilet.

'What about you?' I ask. 'How did it go this morning at the food bank?'

His only reply is to burst out laughing. It's infectious. We can't stop. I don't know why I'm laughing. It's ages since we were helpless with laughter like this, clutching our sides. Since life became such a nightmare, we've lost our smiles. But now, we're laughing. Laughing till we cry. I'm laughing so much that my stomach hurts. Once our fit of laughter's over, still sitting on the toilet, I say:

'Right, now tell me. How did things go there?'

'Finish your business first. Then I'll tell you.'

'Tell me now, it'll make it easier for me.'

A burst of laughter fills the apartment. Ruedi drags a stool over to the bathroom doorway and finally decides to tell me what happened.

They were all there, the many needy with their long faces, crammed into a big waiting room. There were so many of them that some had to wait outside. A heavy silence hung over them. A child strapped to its mother's back started bawling at one point. The mother jiggled about, and the child soon went back to sleep. They'd been there for a while. Some people had arrived earlier, before the office opened. You could feel their mounting impatience. All eyes were riveted on the little raised platform at the front of the vast waiting shed. There was a sea of bags filled with basic necessities: pasta, rice, oil, salt, sugar, canned foods of all kinds, some fresh fruit and vegetables, soap and other essentials.

A few long minutes after the food bank opened, an unassuming-looking woman appeared. She started handing out parcels, yelling people's names in alphabetical order and giving them a bag filled with provisions. A food bank donation. Once they'd been given their life-saving parcels, the recipients quickly left. Perhaps they were ashamed, comments Ruedi. Perhaps they rushed off because they were hungry, I suggest. Ruedi nods in agreement. But should people be ashamed of being hungry? he asks.

I'm still sitting on the toilet. Ruedi laughs. He complains about the smell that's beginning to invade the apartment. I tell him that when you love someone, you love everything about them. Torture, he complains. He gets up from his stool and goes to open the dining-room windows. He picks up a sheet of paper and uses it as a fan.

Another fit of uncontrollable laughter.

He returns to his stool and continues his account.

At one point, the good woman in charge of handing out the food parcels calls his name. Or rather, my name. Yes, my name because the food bank voucher was in my name. The people from Caritas had given it to me the day before. The unassuming woman said: Mwana Matatizo. Ruedi rose and went to get the parcel containing the precious provisions. People stared at him. They looked at him disapprovingly. Very. How could a young white man, red-haired like my Ruedi, have such a strong Bantu-sounding name? Mwana Matatizo. No. There are no redheads in Switzerland with a name like that. Even the food-bank lady looked at him suspiciously. There was something fishy going on. But no one's too fussed when giving crumbs to the poor. To the genuine poor. Because to sink so low, to the level of the food bank, you have to be not only poor but also meek. And Ruedi appeared to have both those traits. So, she let him take his share of food and scurry away like everyone else.

Ruedi has laughed himself out. He's completely forgotten his fan and the smell that's pervading the apartment.

10

This is the first weekend that I'm spending in Lugano with my mother, who's now in San Salvatore private hospital. She's fighting tooth and nail against the disease that's consuming her. That disease is cancer.

I hadn't seen Mama for almost five years. Just regular phone calls. Nothing more. The last time I saw her was in our new house in M'bangala. I say the new house because we hadn't always lived in M'bangala. We had to flee our native M'Fang. But that's another story.

On our last visit back home, at the end of 2002, Monga Minga threw a big party in our honour, Kosambela and me. Hundreds of people gathered in our new house, the one Mama had been able to build thanks to her hard work, but most of all thanks to the money we sent from Switzerland. People came flocking in large numbers, not only from our region of exile, but also from the neighbouring villages.

As well as the big party, news of which echoed even in the far-off villages of M'bangala, I have several happy memories of that last visit. I remember Kosambela, homesick, who spent her time stuffing herself on mangos, the juice running down her arms to her elbows. I remember the woman we affectionately call Auntie

Botonghi. Thrusting out her chest, she boasted of our supposed success in Europe, because she was the one who'd welcomed my sister and me into her home in Geneva. She treated us as if we were her own children because she herself hadn't had any. Best of all, I remember Monga Minga, an elegant, beautiful, joyous, energetic woman. Fulfilled. She had reinvented herself since our departure from M'Fang. Now, she worked. She earned a little something. Not a lot . . . anyway, what did it matter! The main thing for her was having a job. The rest of the gombo, she'd receive directly from Switzerland.

Today, on the train taking me to Lugano, I'm wondering what Mama looks like. I wonder whether she's still the same beautiful, joyous woman that she was five years ago in M'bangala. I have my own idea on the state of things – Kosambela hinted at it a few days ago over the phone. She also revealed things that Mama had been careful to hide from me. For instance, she hadn't told me that the little sore throat that was nothing at all was much more serious. That the pain persisted. That it had obstructed her throat. That she could no longer swallow anything. Anything at all. That she was growing noticeably thinner. That she'd ended up losing her job. That her throat was completely blocked. Blocked-blocked. That the workings were now stalled, paralysed. And on top of all that, there was pain. That the disease had persisted in spite of the remedies of the doctas who practise the Whites' medicine and those of the doctas who practised the medicine of Bantuland.

In general, I know that our Bantu mothers love to exaggerate everything. We even call them drama queens! If there were a ranking of the world's best drama queens, there's no doubt that Mama would come top. She knows how to add salt and spice to every sauce. With her, a simple mosquito bite can easily turn into a venomous mamba bite. A slight headache can become meningitis. How many times has she phoned me, breathless as a marathon runner at the end of the race, to tell me that she's had a serious road accident when someone had merely scratched her rear light? How many times has she told me that such-and-such an aunt was at death's door when in fact the aunt in question was simply suffering from a benign little bout of malaria? And that time when she'd almost given me a heart attack telling me that they'd amputated her foot in the hospital, when in reality they'd simply cut out an ingrowing toenail.

A truckload of questions were going round in my mind. Why hadn't Mama wanted to exaggerate this time? Why hadn't she added spice, sugar, salt and even ginger to her sauce? Why? A thousand 'why's that I also hurled at Kosambela, accusing her of keeping things from me. Her only reply was that this was not the moment to ask questions, but to pray. Just pray, *fratellino*, she said.

At any rate, if Mama had told me the honest-honest truth about her illness, I doubt I'd have believed her any more. I know very well that she's a drama queen. An exaggerator. And besides, don't we all get sore throats? They always clear up by themselves eventually. Nothing to get into a mutton stew about. And hadn't Mama herself told me that Nzambe would help her? Nzambe, Elolombi and the Bankoko would help her because they never forget their children down here on earth. Hadn't Mama herself told me that she'd take a herbal medicine from back home, made of leaves gathered from our sacred forests? She'd even allowed herself a little joke about her illness: it makes me lose weight, she'd boasted. Then she'd added: no need to complicate my life with lemon-carrot-whatsit diets any more. We'd laughed, as usual.

Here, on the train taking me to her this evening, I tell myself that I should have paid more attention to that voice, so hoarse and phlegmy, pretending to be well. But Mama hadn't wanted to say more. She preferred to dwell on Ruedi and on his and my differences. We talked about his too-white skin that can't bear the sun and mine, completely black, that scares the sun. We talked about the Bantuland politicians, about their corruption, their secret bank accounts here in Switzerland, about inflation, devaluation, the rainy seasons, mosquitoes, mangos, the dry seasons, dust, conjunctivitis, oranges, the cold, snow, about gombo to be sent . . .

I'm greeted by a dim light when I walk into Mama's hospital room. From the doorway, I see Kosambela's form. She's wearing a headscarf and has her rosary in her hand. She's sitting on a chair at Mama's feet. It's Mwana, says my sister, watching me come into the room. Oh, my son! cries Mama. I quickly recognise that voice. It's the same one that I'd grown used to hearing over the phone.

I tiptoe over to her bed. It's as if something's holding me back. Am I scared? What should I be scared of?

Mama is lying there, her expression veering between joy and despondency. She smiles. She smiles at me. She gets up and sits on the edge of the bed. She holds her arms out to me. I hug her. She presses me to her as close as she can. We remain locked together for a few moments. I close my eyes, fighting back my tears. This is what is left of my beautiful Monga Minga... she's no more than this. She looks like nothing more than this. The 'this' that I'm holding tight in my arms.

'How are you?' I manage to whisper.

'We're waiting to hear what they say.'

'What have they said?'

'Drop your questions, please,' Kosambela interrupts.

Mama gets back into bed. She doesn't take her eyes off me. I'm distressed to see her in this condition. I so wish I could have seen her otherwise – the same as when I'd left her in M'bangala.

'You're barely in the room and you start your questioning. Are you from the police?' asks Kosambela.

Out of nowhere, a little silence falls on us. Then Mama bursts out laughing. A fit of laughter in the hospital ward. Mama says that Kosambela will always be a Bantu warrior woman. Does snow turn a person white inside? asks Kosambela by way of a reply. We carry on laughing.

When we stop laughing, my sister asks to say a little prayer for Mama: 'Oh eternal God, you made it possible for your servant to come to this country where the doctas and medicine are better than in Bantuland. And it is you who will also enable her to go home in good health. She will bear witness to your goodness throughout Bantuland and elsewhere.' We say amen.

Kosambela rises from her chair. She kisses Mama on the forehead and apologises for having to leave. I haven't seen my sons since yesterday, she offers by way of an excuse. And you there, she says to me as she closes the door behind her, you stop asking so many useless questions. I pull a face. Mama laughs. You can see she's happy to have her children with her. And it's best that way. Whatever happens now, at least we'll be by her side to support her.

Mama says she's a little tired. I'm a little *fatigata*, she says. We dissolve into laughter again. *Fatigata*, *fatigato*, we'll get into the habit of saying it, she and I. We are truly *fatigato*.

I go and sit in the chair that my sister has vacated. A silence sets in between Mama and me. We look at each other for a long while. Neither of us speaks again. As if we had nothing to tell each other. As if we saw each other all the time and we both knew everything about each other's life.

Mama has wasted away. It's frightening. The tumour in her throat has prevented her from eating properly for several weeks. Her eyes are a pale white. The dim lighting makes her look even more corpse-like. Her skin is dull. Darker. Dry. It hangs off her bones.

Not a word. I hold her hand that's not on the drip. I stroke it while gazing at a little painting just above her bed depicting the Holy Virgin Mary with her little boy who never grows up. There's also a crucifix next to it. It's gilded. A machine for I-don't-know-what makes a dripping sound, second after second. Plop, plop, plop. A television suspended in a corner of the room broadcasts a Catholic mass. It's such a long time since I've followed one. On that side of the room, there's a bay window with a sliding door onto a balcony. From there, you can see the bell tower of San Salvatore.

'How is your work placement going?' Mama breaks the silence.

'Still the black sheep.'

'What?'

'Never mind. I'll tell you all about it another time.'

Mama frowns. I could have given her a different answer. A more detailed, fuller one. But no, I didn't feel like talking about that now. I don't feel like talking, full stop. Mama looks at me and smiles. I look down.

She says: 'Honestly, the Whites will never stop amazing me.'

'What do you mean?'

'Now they even have internships for black sheep.'

We laugh. I don't know what to say to her. I don't have the energy or the desire to start telling her all about this sheep business. I simply laugh with her.

'And apart from the black sheep, how's your job-hunting going?'

'It'll be all right. Right now it's hard going.'

'May Nzambe help you, you and your sister. It seems as if this country isn't made for you.'

'Mama . . .'

'When things get too hard, you have to ask for help from the ancestors.'

She tries to sit up. I help her by putting the pillows behind her back. Then, with a remote control, I raise the top half of her bed.

I go over to open the sliding window to let some fresh air into the room.

'With no work and no money, what do you do for eating?' she asks.

'I've still got some of the pumpkin-seed cakes you sent and also some cassava,' I lie.

'You still have that tchop left?! But don't you and Ruedi want to eat or what? Look how thin you are! You have to eat! I sent you all that tchop so you can eat and have the energy to go and look for work.'

'You're the one who most needs to eat, Mama.'

I move a little closer to her. I rest my arm next to hers and say:

'Look, who's the thinnest of us two, you or me?'

A brief silence as we look at our two arms and compare them, then we burst out laughing. Mama laughs so hard that her mirth turns into a coughing fit. I shut up. I stop laughing. I hold her hand again and try to reassure her.

The cough. The phlegm. A lot of phlegm. A little blood. I pass her some wipes. She coughs up her guts. She tries to speak. Her voice refuses to cooperate. Cough! Cough! Everything's obstructed. She touches her throat and gesticulates. Lots of gesticulations that could mean anything. A lump? A burn? A growth? A ligament? Maybe all of those at once. All that in her throat.

I look around for a glass of water to give her. I see one on her bedside table. I pass it to her. That will relieve her a little. I hold out the glass. She glances at me, briefly but intensely. What's happening? It's only a glass of water... Of course! What an idiot I am! Stupid sheep! Mama can't swallow. Cough! Cough! Her throat's completely clogged! Completely clogged. It'll take me a while to grasp that. She can no longer swallow anything. Phlegm comes out, quantities of it. But nothing goes down. Horrible.

Mama stops coughing. I sit back down beside her. Again, I hold her hand that doesn't have a drip attached to it. I stroke it. If only I could cure her with this simple gesture . . . I don't believe in miracles. But who knows? Maybe the Bankoko can fly to her aid.

My eyes sweep over her body. I notice her skin. She has aged. It's like the skin of an old woman, even though Mama isn't even fifty yet. She's only forty-eight. I feel tears welling up again. I fight them back. This is no time to cry, I tell myself.

A profound silence. Awkwardness. We avoid each other's eyes. I pretend to be looking at the machine that's making a noise like water dripping. I pretend to look at the crucifix, the Virgin and her son. I even pretend to watch the mass being served up on the television. I wonder what it's like when you can't eat anything. Can't drink. What it's like having a mouth that's purely decorative? Just a mouth-mouth. Does your saliva dry up? It must taste dull. What am I saying? There's probably no taste. Your tongue is probably annoyed all the time. Your teeth must be bored to death.

Mama starts coughing again. She coughs hard, very hard. I'm panic-stricken. I hold her firmly. I can't let that cough finish her off in front of me. All that gunk buried in her throat comes out in one go. She spews it into a disposable kidney dish. That's it, I say to myself, her mouth is no longer any use for anything but vomiting and spitting.

I suggest calling a nurse. Mama shakes her head. It's always like this, and then it's finished, she says. I stay close to her. I put my arms around her. I hold her very tight, and she says: Ouch! Don't squeeze me so hard or you might suffocate me before this nasty cancer does.

Mama's always joking.

A little later, I ask her how she has been able to cope for almost two months without eating. She repeats that Nzambe and the other gods never forget their children. She tells me that she hasn't let the disease get the better of her. That what's more she never will. She tells me that for days, she chewed and chewed the same piece of meat in the hope of getting it to go down into her stomach. She tried to swallow a tiny piece with a little water, but nothing went down. She had to throw it all up. She contented herself with chewing. Just chewing and feeding on the smell, the taste of the meat, vegetables or cassava. That was all she could still do with her mouth, other than spit. Just the lovely taste of cassava, in my mind, went down to my stomach, she says. There's a tear in the corner of my eye. It plops and trickles down my cheek. I'm not crying. Mama must keep fighting. No tears at the front. Be brave. Cry later, far away, a long way from the hospital, a long way from Mama, a long way from the disease.

What could have caused her to get cancer? I've never seen Mama with a cigarette. Alcohol? A glass of palm wine every so often. Like everyone else. Nothing special. Pollution? Maybe. Who knows how things were at her workplace in M'bangala. One thing that's certain is that Mama didn't work in the fields. She was supposed to be protected from all the chemicals that might have been sprayed from the air. She worked in an office as secretary to the production manager. She was in an old building, a relic from colonial times. When she was at work, she spent all day in a closed, air-conditioned office, behind an ancient computer.

A nurse comes in. She says *buona sera*. We reply *bonna soira*. The woman winces. She says things we don't understand. She's speaking in Italian. She talks so fast. *Non comprendere*, we reply. She speaks more slowly, embellishing her words with descriptive movements. We then understand that she wants to change the drip. I want to ask questions about the why's of all these needles, but the nurse is bound not to understand me.

When the nurse has finished pricking Mama, she says ciao. Ciao, we bleat. *Bonna nuita*, adds Mama.

'That's not how you say it,' I correct her.

'Leave me alone,' she replies. 'You should have said your piece when she was here.'

I ask Mama how she manages to sleep. Which side does she lie on? Left? Right? On her back? On her stomach? What position does she lie in at night?

'The four drips you see there? That's nothing compared to what I had yesterday morning.'

Monga Minga simply laughs. She goes on.

'You should have seen me yesterday. I had ten!'

And that's how it was all day long.

'Yes, ten. Aha! No, fifteen even. Ah, I see. Twenty, you mean. Twenty drips! Wasn't it?'

Laugh. Laughter. That's all I can give Mama this evening.

11

On Saturday morning, Kosambela's kids rouse me from the sofa where I've spent the night. They wake me with their shrieks and kicks. Those little imps, I think, opening one eye. Gianluca, the eldest, and Sangoh, the youngest. Sangoh is the name he's been given in memory of my father. Halfway through giving birth, Kosambela Matatizo herself said to her husband: he'll be called Sangoh. Then, knowing that her husband wouldn't appreciate this flagrant lack of consensus on such an important decision, she immediately added: he'll be called Sangoh, it's either that or nothing.

Gianluca and Sangoh are hyperactive kids. From first thing in the morning, they destroy everything in their path. Their room is always a mess. Kosambela has already given up. She says that these children are beyond her. But I know that once a week she makes them tidy and clean their room. And that's no joke. I'm not going to break my back twice doing the cleaning, both at the hospital and in your room, she says to them in French. When they refuse to do it, she chases them all round the house, brandishing a wooden spatula. The kids laugh as they run. They yell: Aiuto! Aiuto! When their mother eventually gets hold of them, it's a wallop on the left buttock and bingo, into their room. She calls that the *sculasciata* of the week. The boys put away their toys, complaining. She who laughs last laughs longest, says their mother, with a smile.

This morning, a summer sun bathes the room in its warmth, even though it's now the first days of October. My nephews have no intention of leaving me in peace. They jump from one armchair to another and land on the sofa where I'm still lying. Go away! I shout. They burst out laughing. They jump on my kongolibon. They bang it like a tam-tam. They make fun of my head. They speak in Italian. I don't get a word of it, or hardly. Only *testa*, or *guarda*.

Still beneath my thick blanket, I ask them for cuddles. I speak to them in French, which they understand, but only speak a little. And in their limited French they get me to understand that their teacher told them not to cuddle adults. Stupid bitch, I think. I badly need a pee. I have to go to the toilet. When I get up, my nephews laugh even more.

'*Guarda*, he's in his underpants,' hoots Gianluca.

'A drawing . . . a drawing . . .' says Sangoh hesitantly.

'A nanimated drawing,' says his brother.

They snort, pointing at me.

In the bathroom, I pull on my jeans, which I left there the night before. I head into the kitchen where I find a note written by my sister on the fridge door: 'Their father will come and pick them up at around ten.' I look at the kitchen clock. It's only seven. Another three hours to spend with my boisterous nephews. I don't have time to think about my ordeal when an idea suddenly occurs to me. I know what will calm them down, I think, dashing into the sitting room where they're still bouncing from one armchair to another.

I plonk Gianluca and Sangoh in front of Cartoon Network. What's more, I'm in luck, *Ben 10* is on. It's their favourite. I make them two mugs of Caotina hot chocolate. They refuse them and go into the kitchen and help themselves to crisps. I leave them to it.

While they're glued to *Ben 10* and their crisps, I take advantage of the lull to call Ruedi. I wake him up – I can hear it in his hesitant voice. He yawns mid-sentence. He tells me everything's fine. That he misses me a lot but everything's fine. He says he went back to the food bank the previous day. That we have enough food for the next few days. But no meat, he adds. He tells me that he did have some meat though, the previous evening. He was at Dominique's place and there was fillet of beef with mashed potatoes for dinner. He tells me that Dominique was very nice to him. That he was very happy to see him again. That they had a very good time together. That he's still at his place, in Carouge.

'How's your mother?' he asks.

'She's fine. We just hope that she'll get better.'

'And what do the doctors say?'

'We didn't talk about that.'

I don't want to tell him all the things I saw yesterday. I don't want to tell him that my mother really isn't well at all. He must still be in Dominique's arms. Actually, I insist on speaking to Dominique. That will save me from Ruedi's questions. I get Dominique to promise to invite me to eat fillet of beef too. I'm delighted because it's ages since I've eaten any meat, real meat.

When I go back to see Mama at San Salvatore, she's talking with Docta Bernasconi in the presence of a nurse. Bernasconi smiles at me. There's something special in the way he looks at me. It's a sort of affinity. He recognises me, for sure. I say ciao. Hello, Mwana, he replies. Seeing him there, I imagine that he's the one who'll be looking after Mama. I wonder what Kosambela will think of having her mother under the care of a man married to a man. And the Manager-Sisters, why would they have allowed such a situation to occur? Do they no longer respect their protégée's wishes?

Little does it matter what Kosambela thinks of Bernasconi, he's still one of the best oncologists in the area, in the whole of Switzerland even. We're really lucky that Mama is in his hands. Kosambela ought to understand that if you don't have a dog, you go hunting with a goat, as we say back home. And me, I think Docta Bernasconi is a goat with a good sense of smell and who barks loudly.

Docta Bernasconi speaks several languages. According to my sister, he knows up to eight, including Arabic, Chinese and even Swiss-German. And so, he talks to Mama in French. He tells her they're going to operate on her. Very quickly. Certainly early this afternoon. You are too dehydrated, he says, then adds, we'll have to feed you in a different way. Then he goes into a load of scientific stuff that neither I nor Mama understand. The only thing I grasp is that they're going to put a little ball in her stomach to feed her. A sort of tube with a bag that will replace her stomach which, like her mouth, has become useless.

Before leaving, Bernasconi goes to the trouble of holding Mama's hand. We're going to do our utmost, he whispers. Mama smiles. He waves goodbye to me and takes his leave.

'Do you know that that is Docta Bernasconi?' I ask Mama.

'He's so kind,' she answers. 'It's as if Nzambe himself has sent him to look after me.'

'Does Kosambela know about this business?'

'Eh?! What business?'

'No, because we don't want her coming in here yelling loud enough to wake the dead.'

'But she was here earlier with him. She just went off to do her cleaning.'

Her answer surprises me.

I draw up a chair and sit beside her. I launch straight into the story of Docta Bernasconi's marriage. I tell her that the Sisters of the San Salvatore hospital hadn't hesitated for a second before giving their protégée two weeks' sick leave so she could pray and ask God's forgiveness for having attended such a party. My mother opens her eyes wide.

'Aaah!' she exclaims. 'That's why she was forcing herself to smile earlier.'

'You know how the saying goes: the hen pecks according to the size of her throat. Kosambela's is small in this case.'

'As far as I'm concerned, I don't care who lies with him. I just want to get better. That's all.'

I grab the remote to change the channel. I've had enough of the masses being broadcast all day long. As I channel-hop, I hit on the 12.45 news. The lead story leaves me open-mouthed. Where's that? asks Mama, sitting up in bed. It's in Berne, I reply.

There are images of a demonstration and a counter-demonstration between the pro- and the anti-black sheep. The pro-black sheep belong to the NLM. The party dinosaurs are there. They've come to shout their outrage. They've come to say that this country no longer even respects the fundamental freedom that is freedom of expression. They've come to say that they take ownership of their poster. They've come to re-state their determination to kick out all the foreign black sheep. Facing them, the left-wing movements have come to say what they too think of the controversial poster. The anti-black sheep are there to say that the pros are true-true racists, xenophobes, evil-intentioned, mischief-makers, fascists and even filthy sheep. Separating the two sides, the police, dressed like in action movies, are trying to keep the peace.

'Today's the day we'll find out who put water in the coconut,' I say.

'Which is the strongest side?'

'Drop this subject. It's too heavy for you.'

We're glued to the screen like Gianluca and Sangoh watching *Ben 10*. On the TV, they say that the police are unable to contain the crowd of demonstrators and counter-demonstrators. On Place Fédérale, in front of the Parliament in Berne, all hell breaks loose. One group of men attacks another, kicking them relentlessly. Impossible to tell who's who. All you can see is fighting. Mama punches with the demonstrators. He should have head-butted him first, she says. I don't take any notice of her. A journalist is interviewing demonstrators from both sides. It's a ping-pong game. The leader of the NLM, the one who's said to be rolling in gombo, declares into the journalist's mike: if you're mugged in the street, how can people say to you afterwards that if you hadn't been there, it wouldn't have happened? His supporters applaud wildly. They chant the Swiss national anthem, the Swiss Psalm. All of a sudden, in this reportage mosaic, it's Madame Bauer's turn to be in front of the camera. That's my boss! I exclaim.

Mama listens even more closely. Behind Madame Bauer, you can see her dear friend Khalifa in person and her factotum, Mireille Laudenbacher. They stand guard. We demonstrate peacefully, says Madame Bauer. It is those people who are setting the country ablaze with their public xenophobia, she adds. Behind them, the others nod their agreement.

'And you say all this is simply about a sheep matter?' Mama asks.

'Black sheep.'

'They should come to Bantuland, there are lots and lots of sheep, and not just black ones.'

After we laugh, I explain to Monga Minga the ins and outs of this poster business.

12

This morning, Ruedi showers me with *schätzli*. Ever since we've known each other, he often calls me *schätzli* – my little treasure. Which far from displeases me. But since Monga Minga has been lying in San Salvatore, his *schätzli* have become increasingly frequent, invasive even. Ruedi is still making no effort to find himself a little job that would enable us to make ends meet. My first internship pay cheque arrived a few days ago. Already it's all spent. It went on bills. Basic outgoings: rent, water, electricity, phone. I entreated Ruedi to ask his parents to help us out with a little gombo. I hoped that would reimburse some of what I'd spent to spare us the shame of the food bank. How can a person work full-time, even as an intern, and not be able to feed themselves?

Ruedi adamantly refuses to ask for any help from his parents. They've already paid for his health insurance, whereas my insurance company have just sent me a final payment demand. . . . and he calls me *schätzli*.

I pretend not to look at him. I carry on updating my CV, adding my experience in the association that's campaigning against the controversial poster. I glance at him covertly, running my eyes over his face in profile. He looks like a kid, a teenager. The freckles on his nose and cheekbones soften his face. Only his lovely, unkempt ginger beard is evidence that he is indeed a fully grown man. He smiles at me. His brilliant emerald eyes have the same effect on me as the first time I met him. That's already two years ago. Madness! What would I not have given for Ruedi? I would even have sacrificed all of Bantuland simply to tame that creature, that green-eyed fox. And now I have him here, close to me, with his elongated face and a strange look in his eyes. Impish.

Ruedi comes to sit beside me, and puts his right hand arm across my shoulders. I turn away from my computer. Look at him with an amused grin: now what do you want? I ask him.

He accuses me of being aggressive, of verbal abuse, a lack of affection. He's joking, of course. He claims he only wants to make me feel good and help me forget all the things that have been worrying me lately. He pays me compliments. Compliments of all sorts. He says that I'm his *schätzli* and I've got good teeth. That he wishes he had teeth like that too. He takes my hand in his. Whispers that I'm his *schätzli* and I've got beautiful fingers.

'Oh, I was forgetting,' he interrupted himself. 'I love your hair.'

We snort with laughter.

'Leave me alone now,' I say, turning back to my computer.

Ruedi's studying finance. He wants to work in a bank. Like his father. It's a tradition in their family, banking. Going back three or four generations, there have always been bankers in their family, and Ruedi won't be the one to break with it. He pretends to be a rebel, but in reality, he's just a gentle fox, my beloved Ruedi. He'll become a banker, a trader. And if all goes well, he could even become Bernie Madoff. And what about me, what can I do to help? All I can do is encourage him. I can only support his whims. I let him get on with it. I sow with blood, toil, tears and sweat. The day will come when I will reap. One day, I too will be able to say that I'm the partner of a banker. A Swiss banker if you don't mind. Classy! I'll be the bank of my entire family in M'bangala. Each member will have their expertly managed account in Geneva, Lugano or Zurich. I will shower the entire village with real gombo. Manna in the equatorial desert of our land. How happy I will be to call Ruedi *schätzli*!

While waiting for this hoped-for day of glory, I work my fingers to the bone.

At home, I do my utmost to help. I keep to the housework rota. I cook when it's my turn. I clean when it's my turn – at least when I can: I don't want Kosambela's backache. I iron when it's my turn. I smile too when it's my turn. And of course, I fuck when it's my turn. Ruedi tells me not to worry about all that, that he'll do it all. And now we have food from the food bank, he always asks me: so, my *schätzli*, what do you fancy for dinner tonight?

I am lucky to be with this little fox.

This morning, when Ruedi asks me what I fancy for dinner, I tell him I don't give a shit about his cooking. I say it harshly, almost hurtfully. He treats it as a joke and asks again. Your lentils taste horrible, I reply coldly.

Ruedi goes quiet. The bullet hit home. He seems upset. I got him. I feel like firing another. I feel like aiming my cannon mouth and opening fire. I hold back. It saddens me a little. But it gives me a certain satisfaction. He blushes. I like seeing him red with pain. Perhaps even anger.

Silence distances us from each other a little.

Over the past few weeks, I've been away a lot because I have to go to Lugano to see Mama. He spends a lot of time with Dominique. He has to fill the gaps one way or another. Does it hurt him? He's getting closer to me, for sure. He's trying to be supportive, I can see. But why won't he let his parents help us out? Why won't he get up off his arse and find a job? Why is he content for us to live like beggars? Why does he restrict himself to queueing at the food bank? Why doesn't he do anything to get us out of this mess?

Since Mama has been at San Salvatore, I often take refuge in our bedroom. I let myself get carried away by gloomy thoughts about her uncertain future, her inability to swallow anything, the complicated treatment she's receiving. Recently they inserted a bag in her stomach. This bag should replace her stomach which has had to take a holiday. It's this bag that will feed her now. Feed? That's an exaggeration. They inject into it minerals and other nutritional substances she needs to survive. Her stomach is open. She has a big dressing on it. That's where the tube goes in. It's become her mouth. A tube . . . When I think about all that, I'm overcome by a great sadness. And at those moments, not even Ruedi's *schätzli* can comfort me. I cry and choke back my anguish, thinking of

Mama's throat. And while pain makes its way deep down inside me, on the other side of the wall, in the kitchen, I can hear Ruedi chatting with his mother on the phone. *Cioè.* They laugh. They even roar with laughter. All's well in their world. All's not well in mine.

So how can he try to have me believe, this morning, that he shares my pain. It's not his effusive *schätzli* that will prove it to me. It doesn't matter how much affection they contain. It's not lentil dishes from the food bank that will prove it to me. That's not enough. I want him to bear my cross with me. I want him to drink from the chalice with me. I want him to feel the pain of my crucifixion. I want the thorns in my crown to pierce his skull through to his brain and for drops of blood to ooze from the wound. I want us to share everything, truly everything, like proper companions, like proper partners. Does he not remember what the lady from the register office said when we went there to sign? Does he not remember that she said a partnership is about solidarity? Solidarity! Sharing! Well, if he doesn't remember, then I do! And I'm going to show him.

I leave Ruedi sitting on a chair in our kitchen-living room. He looks downcast. I escape to the kitchen window to smoke a cigarette. I light it. As I take a drag, I savour my beloved companion's hurt. Me too, I feel like smiling, laughing, roaring with laughter. I also want to call my mother and share that laughter with her, but sadly, I know she won't really be able to laugh. She is going from bad to worse. She's just had her first dose of chemotherapy. She's not laughing. She's no longer laughing. She's no longer joking. She won't be able to help me tame my beautiful little fox.

I feel disloyal. I feel brutal, a shit, malign, nasty, unhealthy. I close my eyes for a second and ask Nzambe to forgive me. I open them and I see the housework rota for Ruedi and me on the fridge door:

Laundry:

Ruedi: washing

Mwana: ironing

Cleaning:

Ruedi: bedroom

Mwana: kitchen and bathroom

Flexible depending on availability

Cooking:

Alternate days

Flexible depending on availability

Ruedi gets up and joins me at the window. He smiles again. His smile is a little nervous this time. I hope he won't call me *schätzli*. He doesn't. Phew! I sense his gaze telling me everything's going to be all right. He can't speak words of comfort with his mouth. He must realize that this is not the right time.

In his innocent gaze, I have the feeling that it's Monga Minga talking to me. I look down. He puts his arms around me. The tenderness he displays proves that he truly loves me. It also proves to me that he isn't yet completely affected by the distress that I'm experiencing. But that will come. It will just take a little more time. It will come.

13

I'm in Lausanne. There's a storm brewing. I'm waiting for the train home. Between the screech of a train pulling into the station and the thunderclap heralding the storm, a voice over the PA announces a delay of seven minutes. Passengers around me heave sighs of annoyance. Discontent. Seven minutes, that's really outrageous! Someone on the platform is threatening to send a letter of complaint. I move away from all that. I find a seat on a public bench and have a quiet smoke. A street cleaner comes and sweeps between my legs. He apologises. I smile at him.

Around me: posters. That's where the electoral battle is played out in my cousins' country. That's where they debate, argue, insult or applaud one another, call each other every kind of devil, sheep and black sheep. Beaming mugshots promise change, as usual. They say there'll be a new beginning. That this time, it's for real. That there will be a more justice. More solidarity. A lump-sum taxation regime. Better climate protection. Development of the nuclear industry. A marked improvement in the living standards of the middle classes. Families. Oh, families! Promises to cut family benefits to reduce the burden on the taxpayer. A real drop in unemployment. And also to reduce unemployment benefits. Promises of a stronger country in the face of the invasion, the invasion of foreigners. An extension of the free movement of individuals. But not for all Europeans. The faces on the posters woo the voter. Smiles. Garish colours. Promises. Contradictions. Women. Men. They promise a lot of things. They promise the impossible.

Election posters have taken over the station. The federal elections are being held in one week's time, next Sunday. Our cousins here will be entirely overhauling their parliament, from top to toe. I mentioned it to Mama last Saturday. At first, she said nothing. She's tired these days. I carried on talking about it to try and arouse her curiosity a little because I know she's usually interested in these issues. Then she laughed and asked me to drop it with these stories of liars. No. I told her no. They're not liars. At any rate, not here. Here, it's not like back home in Bantuland. People are people, she pronounced.

At the office, Madame Bauer and company were still galvanised by the sheep of discord. And that sheep still dictated my work life. I will have devoted three months of internship fighting a black sheep. Type up this press release to counter the arguments of the enemy camp. Send a reply to the question of a journalist who wants to add fuel to the fire. Write down a political contribution or speech for a meeting, dictated to me by Madame Bauer as she stubs out her umpteenth cigarette in the overflowing ashtray. Every so often, she comments on a poster on the office wall. This morning, for example, she talked to me about the poster demanding the abolition of bullfighting in Spain. She told me that it is a terrible thing to see an animal die like that, slowly. She told me that the cruellest part was seeing how the crowd clapped until their hands blistered, applauding a death that was so spectacularly drawn out. It's brutal, she says. Then she told me the story of Mireille Laudenbacher who is currently warring with the local authorities to prevent her dog from being put down. It has already cost her some fifteen thousand Swiss francs. I'm gobsmacked. How can a person spend so much on saving a dog?

I ask her for a cigarette, hoping that way to regain my composure.

As well as my writing tasks, I manage our website, which I set up. There's something incredibly interesting about this website, and that's the chat room. Since the demos in Lausanne on 18 September and the battle in Berne of 6 October, our online forum has been exploding with messages. People really let rip:

Simon, 18 September, 20.18: You say you're tolerant? Really! And is setting Avenue Vinet on fire tolerance? You're terrorising everyone. And bravo for your demos, they show us what you're really about: encouraging this country's delinquents.

Karine du Choux-de-Vaud, 19 September, 8.36: This is complete crap. I took part in the Lausanne march. At around 7 p.m. the organisers announced the demo was over. There were more than two thousand of us. We all left peacefully, after simply expressing our indignation at the racist, hate-filled xenophobic violence being spread by the NLM with its billionaire leader. That is a real success! Just a handful of young firebrands who stayed on to protest radically against the excessive barriers and Robocops trained to protect the man who has long been stoking a climate of fear and suspicion among the public.

All together :), 22 September, 12.50: Down with the fucking racists!

Röstigraben, 30 September, 14.12: Why keep these people in our country? THEY MUST GO HOME! These people come here, to our country, they refuse to work, refuse to abide by our laws and on top of that, they live on our money on benefits. Enough's enough! OUT!

Merde, 2 October, 18.15: Dirty lezza!

Madame Bauer doesn't like the messages against her campaign. She doesn't want her opponents coming and cooking in her pot. They can just go and write their comments in their own chat rooms, damn them! she says. Then, this morning, she asked me quite simply to delete all the messages against her. And she was adamant about the particularly offensive messages. Calling her a lezza? That's a bit much!

I spent the whole of today sifting the messages like cassava flour. You have to remove the lumps for the couscous to be smooth. After sifting them all, I posted my first and only message in the chat:

> Admin, 15 October, 17.04: We do not accept offensive comments under any circumstances. If you wish to contribute, refrain from insults and try to present proper arguments.

I was forgetting an important piece of information. I also learned this morning that Monsieur Khalifa was standing for the federal elections. Mireille Laudenbacher even added that this is not his first time as a candidate. She says that he's a good man – humanist and tolerant. And above all, she insists, he loves animals.

At first, I thought it was a joke, because I've never seen a single poster of Monsieur Khalifa in the streets, not in Lausanne or anywhere in the Vaud. He's never been the subject of a controversy. I've never heard him on the radio. I've never seen him on TV, other than standing guard behind his dear friend Madame Bauer. I was really amazed.

But what to do if he really is serious about it?

The train taking me back to Geneva pulls into the station at last. I find a seat in a quiet coach. My Swiss cousins even have compartments where you're not allowed to make a noise. A pictogram showing an index finger pressed against closed lips warns you. I choose a secluded corner seat. I close my eyes to rest them from my long day's work in front of a screen. A scene comes back to mind. At lunch time, when I was on my break, I sat in a little public park to eat the sandwich that Ruedi had made for me the previous day. While I was gazing at the interplay of autumnal colours, I spotted a group of kids on the other side of the park: a school crocodile supervised by three kindly-looking women. They must have been the teachers. They walked right past me kicking the heaps of dead leaves. A little fair-haired girl with glasses gives me a shy 'Bonjour, monsieur'. I smiled at her. I watched the crocodile heading towards the fountain when it came to an abrupt halt. They were staring at a poster . . . That poster again. I hadn't even noticed it earlier. I wondered what the teachers would tell those children, and more importantly, what seven- or eight-year-olds themselves might think of it. They stood there for around a quarter of an hour. I couldn't hear what they were saying. But a light wind carried a few words spoken too loudly: discrimination, racism, bad, the other, foreigners, intolerance, etc.

I barely have the time to go over that scene when a hand lands on me. Who on earth can it be? I am being roused by two young women. They're talking to me. Can't they see we're in a quiet coach?

Safia and Orphélie! Two close friends. We were at uni together. We were in the same year group. We graduated just over a year ago. Since then, we've lost sight of each other, all wrapped up in our own lives, even though we'd been quite close. At the time, we had classes from Mondays to Wednesdays. The rest of the week was ours. Those in charge of our Master's programme said that this timetable gave students a little more time to work, study, write their essays, read, do sports, etc.

On Thursdays and Fridays, I worked for Monsieur Nkamba of Nkamba African Beauty. I was a door-to-door sales rep visiting Black customers to flog a vast range of skin-lightening products. I would often work on Sundays too, in the Revivalist churches. Between lively visits from the Holy Spirit, I'd sell my products. I was successful, and I made a lot of gombo from those ladies' skins.

Like me, Safia was in sales. She worked in a luxury clothes store on Rue du Rhône in Geneva. She must have enjoyed it because fashion was her thing. She always pretended to faint when she saw the outfits of some women in the street. As for Orphélie, she was a waitress in a trendy bar in the Old Town of Geneva. She often complained about her very irregular working hours. She also complained about the disrespectful behaviour of some customers. She was a very beautiful woman, Orphélie. Every year she worked as a hostess at the Geneva Motor Show. At the Watch Fair too. We admired her for that. Whereas I had to work to make a living, and to some extent to provide for my family back in Bantuland, Safia and Orphélie worked purely for themselves, to buy clothes and travel. Their parents provided for them.

Safia and Orphélie are sitting there, opposite me. We had to change compartments. They're so elegant: dark suits, light blouses and shoes with kitten heels. Only Safia's tights stand out and betray her love of fashion. They're lemon-yellow. It's the distinctive touch. Otherwise, the two of them are perfect. Impeccable manicures, subtle make-up and hair in ponytails.

Since leaving uni, I've often thought of them and wondered what they're up to. Promised myself I'd get back in touch. I'd forget, then the idea would surface again. I'd tried once but got an answering machine. I left a message then waited for them to call me back. Radio silence. So, I decided to keep quiet too. I'd hoped to find them on Messenger. But we didn't have internet at home, so I couldn't use that means of communication. And I'd never have taken the liberty of doing it from Madame Bauer's office.

Meanwhile, the storm breaks. The sky suddenly turns dark. The torrential rain lashes the windows of the moving compartment, making a terrible racket. The train slows down every so often and a voice with a German accent gives regular updates on how many minutes late the train is. Around *acht minuten*. Around *nein minuten*. My friends and I don't give a shit about the delay. The longer it is, the more time we'll have to catch up.

We chat. We chat a lot. The girls laugh. They laugh a lot. Some of the other passengers stare at us, but that doesn't bother us. We carry on laughing our heads off. We talk about the dreadful weather and the forecast for the coming days. We talk about natural disasters. We exchange uni stories as if all that was yesterday. We talk about partying at the weekend. We talk about our last-minute revision sessions. We talk about this lecturer or that friend who got on our nerves.

'That guy who taught research methodologies was a real pain,' says Safia.

'What was his name again?' asks Orphélie.

'The tortoise!' I say.

We gently make fun of the bald, stunted tutor with no buttocks – just a continuation of his back – whose slow speech and movements had earned him the nickname of 'the tortoise'.

A few moments' silence come between us. Orphélie glances out of the window where little beads of rain are dancing. Safia adjusts her brooch with big red petals and checks the state of her lemon-yellow tights.

'Wow, girls! You really are soooo classy.'

'Thank you, Mwana,' replies Safia, tucking a strand of stray hair behind her right ear.

We exchange compliments. A fresh silence. A thunderclap. I gaze at Safia's tights or at Orphélie's red lipstick. I admire my former uni friends' stylishness. I look at myself. The contrast is striking. No need to ask what they're up to. They're both successful. It's visible. We are no longer on the same planet. Around *twelf minuten*. The stress of staying on this train sitting opposite these girls is beginning to suffocate me. I want to disappear. I know that if the train is delayed any longer, I'll have to talk about the question – yes, the question! – that I have no wish to discuss. I don't want to talk about myself. I don't have anything interesting to tell them. My life has been nothing but a failure since I left uni. They must have noticed. Otherwise, they'd have asked me the question. Orphélie keeps her eyes fixed on the window. It's as if she's mesmerised by the dance of the rain. And Safia has taken a fashion magazine out of her bag. No, if I don't say something now, we'll be like people who don't know one another. People who've never met. But I don't want it to feel like that during the short time we have left together.

'What are you doing now?' I ask.

Safia answers first. It's as if she's been waiting for that question. She answers almost robotically. She tells me she's just been made head of strategy for a major services company in Lausanne. She says she's been working there for just over four months. That the job fits her like a Gucci glove, and she really loves it. She tells me that she's about to move out of her little studio to an apartment in Geneva's Champel neighbourhood. A gorgeous apartment, she feels compelled to add with a smile. I disguise my surprise, or rather my jealousy. I smile too. I even laugh. Congratulations! I exclaim. We all smile, but only for a few seconds. Then silence threatens once more. Safia opens her mouth again. This time, she sounds defensive:

'But don't you go thinking I just walked into the job. It wasn't easy at all. Not at all. I had to send off loads of applications all over the place, make several calls. Not to mention attending interviews. But it was always no. But I kept at it. Then, one day, I was in the right place at the right time.'

Orphélie tells me she works for a bank. In the events and communications department, she says. She manages the funding applications for cultural events. She's quite vague about the rest. She won't say any more. No need to. Whatever she says, people will always suspect she was helped by her father, a senior executive in another major bank. Orphélie simply concludes by saying that she really has found her dream job.

'What about you, what are you up to, Mwana?' asks Orphélie, moving on.

The dreaded question.

'Me? Umm . . .'

What can I say to them? What should I say to them after everything they've told me? I'm ashamed.

They seem so far removed. Right then, I think of Monga Minga. When I was little, she always used to say to me: sheep may flock together, but they don't have the same price.

'I'm doing an internship with a very large, internationally renowned association. It's an organisation that combats racial discrimination and promotes diversity and multiculturalism around the world.'

'Wow! That's interesting! What's the name of this organisation?'

A moment's hesitation and solitude. The ground gives way beneath me.

'WPLO,' I say eventually. 'World Peace and Love Organisation.'

'What . . . ?'

'You two won't have heard of it. They've only just opened their Lausanne office. Look on Wikipedia and you'll find it.'

'OK.'

They don't appear convinced.

'Are you enjoying it?' asks Safia.

'Oh, I love it! It's really cool. OK, I'm overloaded. I'm anxious all the time because there's so much stuff to be done. But it's really ace.'

'And how long does it last?'

'What?'

'Your internship.'

'It's for a year, renewable. And given all the projects I'm working on right now, it's clear they're going to take me on. It's definite. They've even confirmed it already. There's the funding for it. Yeah, I'm really happy. I've found my dream job.'

'Brill. I'm really happy for you,' says Safia.

'You deserve it,' adds Orphélie.

I had mentioned discrimination. The girls ask me if my World Peace whatever had noticed the sheep posters. This question feels like pressure. I sense a river of sweat soaking my armpits. If they carry on with their questions, I'm likely to explode. But I calm down.

'Oh yes!' I reply. 'They've noticed those posters. But they've got lots of other concerns. They deal more with international discrimination. The sheep aren't really their thing. They're looking at the big picture.'

The girls don't seem too convinced. But still they smile. They congratulate me.

The train pulls into Geneva station around *achteen minuten* late. I say goodbye to Safia and Orphélie and we exchange phone numbers. We make lots of promises that we know we'll never keep. We're politicians too, except we don't have posters.

When I turn into the street where I live, I feel tears welling up. Tears. Why cry? Rage. Against whom? Against what? They haven't done anything to you. Of course, they haven't done me any harm. But the tears are there. Maybe they're tears of joy. Yes. Most likely. Because I'm proud of myself. I played the game. I did what had to be done. I played the game. That's how it is: you have to act as if . . . I wasn't going to tell them that I was doing a three-month work placement in a tiny, stupid NGO that had found nothing better to focus on than a nice little black sheep. I wasn't going to go on about all my woes, was I? No. I wasn't going to tell them that I sometimes went hungry. That I only ate thanks to the food bank. That even the food banks were beginning to be sick of the sight of us, Ruedi and me. I wasn't going to tell them that my mother has terminal cancer that's decided to reside in her throat. I wasn't going to tell them that my sister and I had a bill of six thousand francs to pay – only six thousand francs! – a little bill that the Manager-Sisters see fit to charge us. No. I wasn't going to tell them that I get paid an intern's salary which is only enough to allow me to stay a few more months in the shitty apartment where I live with my boyfriend. I wasn't going to tell them that in a few short weeks, at the end of my internship, I might end up on the streets because I won't be able to afford my rent any longer, was I? No. No. I wasn't going to tell Safia that all my job applications – oh, how many have I made?! – all my efforts to find a job, routinely result in a resounding failure that sends icy shivers down my spine. I wasn't going to tell them all that, was I? No. I wasn't going to drop my trousers in front of them. I had a package in front, for sure, but behind . . . life was fucking me up the arse. And that's not a pretty sight. I didn't want to show them. You're either Bantu or you're not! I have my pride to preserve! I am a Bantu. All the same! Even when the river's dry, it must keep its name.

The tears finally flowed. I lowered my head so as not to attract attention. I clenched my jaw to keep down the pain that was tearing me apart. Safia! Little Safia. Orphélie! I cry. I'm still crying when I open the door to my apartment. My beautiful red-headed Ruedi greets me and puts a little sunshine in my head. I cry even harder . . .

14

Monga Minga was born in a little village in the northwest of Bantuland, in the heart of the M'fang forest. She showed an interest in acting from a very early age. At the beginning of the Sixties, the very new Bantuland administration and its military leader had made culture one of their priorities. It was an effective means of educating the masses, and also helped to create and maintain national unity. Plays with a strong educational content were put on throughout the country. Depending on the region, the actors spoke French, English or Portuguese.

At fifteen, after gaining her elementary school certificate, Monga Minga had gone into the theatre. Her parents were scandalised. She was of the age to marry and start a family. But Monga Minga dreamed of something different. She had dug her heels in. She didn't see herself ending up like those young women in her village, her breasts floppy and permanently in the mouth of a toothless infant. She had her primary school certificate under her belt. That was all you needed in those days to join the ranks of the civil service. With no entrance exam, Monga Minga had become an actor. She travelled the length and breadth of the M'fang region and even far beyond, across the whole of Bantuland as she'd always wanted, preaching the message of the New Bantu Administration in every village.

Monga Minga often used to tell Kosambela and me stories about her theatrical performances. Huge crowds would gather around a tiny stage protected by a few soldiers armed to the teeth. The mission of the state-official-actors was to promote respect for the military authorities, but primarily to condemn tribalism. The audience laughed until they cried. Perhaps because they identified with the characters. Or perhaps because they didn't give a damn. Now, Mama says that ultimately the message didn't get across: since the Sixties, tribalism has remained intact in Bantuland.

In the Eighties, the New Bantu Administration decided to slash its culture budget. It needed to increase army salaries, since coups d'état were in vogue. Actors' pay was reduced by two thirds. To live with dignity, Monga Minga had no option but to get married. And besides, at her age, she had no intention of remaining single. She was twenty-one and she didn't yet have a child. She would like to have had one, even without getting married!

For her family, she was the embodiment of shame.

Nzambe had her cross paths with a man called Sangoh Matatizo. A soldier. His salary hadn't been reduced. And he made good gombo. Nice shiny, regular pay. The lifespan of the New Bantu Administration depended on the army, and therefore on him.

One by one, the theatre stages disappeared from the villages. Most of the actors had found other work. Only a few passionately committed individuals had withstood the wage cuts and continued to serve the Christian nation. The others had gone back to their hoes, their machetes and their hunting spears. They went back to being farmers, or petty officials or even taxi drivers. Monga Minga was one of the rare actors to carry on. She wasn't short of money. After all, wasn't her husband in the military?

I myself glided through childhood on my father's gombo. In Bantuland, when you're the son or daughter of a soldier, you can walk with your head held high and your chest thrust out. Hey, you! Do you know who I am? I'm not just anybody! I'm the son of a soldier. I do as I please, when I please and where I please. My father's military protection enveloped me. Even at school, the teachers stood to attention! They knew who they could horse-whip. They readily beat the children of others, the children whose parents didn't pose a threat. Whereas I . . . I had all that was necessary to earn the respect of my teachers and even of the head teacher. Military protection. You dare raise a hand to me and my father will declare war on you.

I remember once, my sister Kosambela had gone to the extreme of insulting the head teacher of our school, who'd scolded her, justifiably, for not having done her homework. Kosambela hadn't been able to stomach the reprimand. After all, she was the daughter of a soldier. So, she felt entitled to hurl abuse at the head, who was alarmed and summoned Monga Minga and Sangoh. Reason: bad behaviour. Sangoh had grown angry. Very angry. At first, he did his utmost to lock up the head who had dared accuse his daughter of bad behaviour. Then, back home, he thrashed Kosambela with his belt. Monga Minga screamed. Aieee, don't kill my daughter! Please, husband, don't kill my daughter! But Papa took no notice. He was well aware that his wife was an actor. When Papa carried on beating Kosambela's buttocks, Monga Minga leaped onto his back and bit his right ear. He yelled like a palm rat caught in a trap.

Last night, in Mama's hospital room in San Salvatore, we recalled that incident. We laughed about it. The nurses asked us to keep our voices down. Monga Minga can't really laugh because the balloon they've put in her stomach won't let her give a proper belly laugh worthy of an actor of her calibre. So, she merely gave little gasps. As for Kosambela, she laughed heartily. Good. That allowed her to forget her backache for a while. She doesn't really like me telling stories like this, because she's changed a great deal since then. Now she's the daughter of Nzambe and is never without her headscarf or her rosary.

Sangoh's absences grew more frequent. There were rumours in the village that he had a mistress. It wasn't exactly front-page news. In those days, what man in any village could deny having a spare wheel? What man in our village could claim to eat only his cassava and nothing but his cassava every day? Sangoh's mistress was one of Mama's closest friends: the woman we still call Auntie Botonghi with great affection, even now. Auntie Botonghi was a beautiful, modern woman who was pampered by her husband. Mama knew that Auntie

Botonghi enjoyed Papa's spicy plantain. Everyone knew. But Mama turned a blind eye. It wasn't her friend's fault, she was convinced of that. And anyway, what woman from our village could complain about her husband's straying? There's a saying back home that the man is outside, like his sex, and the woman is inside. Mama agreed to share Papa with her best friend. After all, in the event of polygamy, there would be fewer problems. The snag is that Botonghi was the wife of one of Papa's military colleagues, no more and no less! Does a guy mess around stealing the wife of a soldier?

One evening, the cuckolded husband caught Sangoh carrying out his army drill on his wife Botonghi. He whacked him hard on the back of his neck. A killer blow. Sangoh departed thus, in action on the battlefield. He departed thus, leaving Mama, Kosambela and me with no more military protection. He departed thus. Without so much as a proper goodbye!

Auntie Botonghi was cast out. The disgrace of the village, people said, their voices full of hypocrisy. Oh shame, oh shame! The woman who brought misfortune on our village. As the fury of the village came down on her, she used the last of her savings to flee to Switzerland, to Geneva. Auntie Botonghi knew that Geneva was the refuge of all the army dissidents (the black sheep, my father Sangoh would have called them).

In the village, people had accused Mama of killing her husband. If she'd stood up for herself, Sangoh wouldn't be dead, they said. That's what they thought, those village women who also said that a man can't eat rice every day.

We were driven out of the area. We fled to the M'bangala region, across the Ubangi River. Mama had no choice. She had to end her acting career. If she had stayed there, waiting for someone to pay her the gombo of her deceased husband, she'd have festered in the sun! Armed with her primary school certificate, she eventually found a job as a supervisor on a banana plantation in the north of Bantuland.

A few years later, probably to redeem herself, Auntie Botonghi had agreed to have my sister and me come to live with her in Geneva.

And now, Monga Minga is here, staying in our cousins' country. She has a kongolibon like mine. Maybe she'd dreamed of going to Europe one day. Her patch of Europe is now reduced to a hospital ward. Without antibodies. Without any military protection. She can rely only on Docta Bernasconi and his team. She's relying on Nzambe, Elolombi and above all the Bankoko among whom Papa now belongs.

15

The replies are still negative. For over a year, I haven't been offered a single interview. It's depressing. It's painful. It's stinging. It's exhausting. I feel stupid. No good for anything. Like Mama's mouth, incapable of doing anything. Each rejection feels like a slap in the face. And there are a lot of them.

Before, on receiving those negative replies, I'd call to ask for feedback on the reasons why I'd been rejected. It was also a way of showing how keen I was. Of making an impression. In a brutally sober and calm tone, the person I spoke to would explain that they'd been inundated with hundreds and hundreds of applications. That it had been a very difficult choice. That I, like many other applicants, fulfilled all the requisite criteria. That I had an excellent profile. That I had a very good track record, excellent training. That my experience as a sales rep was perfect, that this and that made me an outstanding applicant... but there had been someone better qualified than me. There were so many better qualified than me that I couldn't even be shortlisted. No one wanted to see me, receive me, hear me, give me a chance, hear how motivated I am. What if they'd at least invited me for an interview? And what if they'd then said no? How would

I have taken it? Would I have come out of it stronger, motivated or, on the contrary, diminished?

One day, while I was typing up a press release that Madame Bauer had given me, my phone rang. I didn't recognise the number that flashed up. It was a landline. When that happens, I'm always torn between excitement and resignation. I feel excited at the thought that this call might be from a potential employer inviting me to an interview. But that excitement always turns into resignation. My disappointment is often huge when I realise it's simply a telesales call offering me a product for which I have absolutely no need. Then I swear at them and hang up abruptly. Bunch of frauds!

But that day was different. On the other end of the line was a human resources lady from a company I'd applied to. For the first time in a year, my heart leaped with anticipation. The human resources lady told me that she'd received my application. That they were interested. She offered me an interview. We set a date. After which I let out sighs of victory. It seemed like a done deal. No way would I miss this unique, desperately awaited opportunity. A huge breath of fresh air. A rebirth. A resurrection. I could already see myself in my new job, happy. No more black sheep. Goodbye, Madame Bauer and company. I'll look up all my old uni friends to tell them that I've finally found something. A real something. I'll stand up straighter. I'll shrug off my loser attitude and adopt that of the chosen. The transformation will be so striking that everyone around me will notice. I'll go to Lugano to tell my mother that our trials and tribulations are now over. That I will pay for some of her hospital costs. That the Manager-Sisters of San Salvatore hospital can now keep their charity. I'll be able to pay for Kosambela's backache treatment. I'll be able to take my nephews to the Circus Knie where they'll see elephants and dogs dancing the Bantu rumba. Now I'll be able to go to the Grison Alps to see Ruedi's family and say to them: 'Hey! You don't need to help us out any more. I've found an *Arbeit*.' I'll be able to do all that, I will. Freedom.

I called Ruedi. He cooked lentils and vegetables to celebrate. We could see our life changing.

The next day, at dawn, I received an email from the human resources lady. Surely an employment contract or at least confirmation of our upcoming meeting. Well, no . . . This lady had emailed me to say that she'd confused me with another applicant. She spoke of a mistake. I wasn't the person she wanted to interview. She apologised profusely for this inconvenience. She cancelled our meeting. She sincerely wished me the best of luck in finding employment.

After so many years of studies and specialisation, I'm still not the right person. There's always someone better qualified than me. And that must be true. Well, I suppose so. It's not as if there's a lack of talent. There must be people who are better qualified than me. If that's what they tell me, then it must be true. Especially when it's said in a calm, very calm, sympathetic voice. It's reassuring. It gives me a little hope. The people I meet or who I call sound so pleasant, so empathetic, so kind and then so cutting. Their voices are simultaneously wounding and healing. They stab and staunch. They rip and soothe. They offend and flatter. I have the ideal profile, for sure, but not the right one. At any rate, not this time. Even less next time. I'll have to try again another time. Have faith.

I think I'm getting used to it. I know those words of rejection by heart. Before, they went through me like a knife, diminishing me, bruising me, vilifying me, but now, when I receive them, I read them out loud, recite them in a comical, tragi-poetic voice. I laugh uproariously at them. I roll on my kitchen floor. I tear the rejection letter into a thousand pieces, toss them in the air and let them rain down on me. I laugh at my fate. I laugh at my stupidity. I laugh at my madness. I cry. Then I eat lentils to forget.

There's no way out. It reminds me of the mirror in the lift at the unemployment office. The mirror that mocks you and keeps reminding you that you'll never move on. And it's true. I'll never move on. They must be right. I don't have the right profile. I'm not what they're looking for. I'll probably never be what they're looking for. I'll never come up to their expectations. I'll never manage it. But what am I saying? I'm losing my mind. Will I really never manage it? No. Come on. One day. Never.

Recently, Monga Minga told me that she'd heard on the radio in her hospital room that unemployment levels had gone down again in Switzerland. That the politicians of all stripes were pleased with themselves. I made no comment. Didn't want her to start going on about me not trying hard enough, maybe I complain too much. When I tell her that it's tough, she replies: the hyena that does nothing but howl will never catch its prey. You have to keep at it, she says. Perhaps she's right. The unemployment figures have fallen even lower these past three months. I also read that at the office. It was Madame Bauer who passed me the newspaper, folded back at the page where that article was. I don't know why. Was it to mock me or to encourage me? Switzerland had one of the lowest rates in Europe, around three per cent. In Paris, Berlin and Rome, they're falling over themselves to strangle unemployment. Here, among our Swiss cousins, it is quietly dying out, all by itself, without any obvious effort being made. But me, I still have to wait.

Monga Minga asked me how others managed? How do they do it, then? she asked me in a profoundly surprised voice. She asked me how those young graduates they talked about on the TV every day managed it? How do they do it, the ones who just a few months after finishing their studies are already employed? How do they do it? How did my friends Safia and Orphélie do it? The right time? The right place? The right application documents? The right letter? The right contact? How did they do it, those in my year group who have managed to find a real something? Do they have a thousand years of professional experience under their belt? . . . Nzambe only knows.

Beside my bed there's a class photo taken at the Master's graduation ceremony. It's a lovely photo, which I treasure. For me it's a trophy that bears witness not only to my university career here among my cousins, the Swiss, but also to the friendships forged over years. For this ceremony, I bought myself a dark suit like the kind you wear on important occasions. I remember that Kosambela and Auntie Botonghi were there. I remember the moment when the dean of our faculty called out my name, Mwana Matatizo. He didn't pronounce it properly, but it didn't matter. People applauded, half-heartedly. My sister Kosambela and Auntie Botonghi, from the back of the room where they'd arrived late with my two nephews, let out a loud Bantu ululation. The entire auditorium turned around to stare at them. They didn't take the slightest bit of notice. They carried on yelling as women do in our village: youyouyouyouyouyou! youyouyouyouyou! I was full of shame.

I smile at the memory.

A copy of the photo I'm holding had been sent to Bantuland, to the M'bangala region where my mother had fled. I had become her pride and joy. Her son, a graduate from a Whites' university.

It was the recognition. Kosambela, who accused her ex-husband of lacking respect for her because she hadn't studied for years like him, now had a new argument of substance: she had a brother with a degree from the University of Geneva.

Kosambela hadn't appreciated Ruedi's presence at the ceremony. She hated him. But she was so proud of me that she preferred to ignore the interloper. She wanted to relish that moment, she who'd opted for marriage over studying.

When I think of all those moments, I smile. I tell myself that everything will be all right. I look at the photo in my hands again. In it, I have a radiant smile. I'm filled with pride. I open my bedside drawer to put away this souvenir photo. A collection of rejection letters stares up at me. A load of bumph. The bumph of despair. My shoulders droop. When will the day come when I'll be in the right place at the right time? That day will definitely come. I'll make it. One day. I stay hopeful. One day. But when? I don't know . . . a bit later, perhaps. Definitely. It's first come first served. Those who come from elsewhere have to wait. I must wait my turn. I must push too. Push, but most importantly, be patient.

Supposing I went back to Bantuland? That's one solution. I was forgetting. With my degrees, I'd most likely be valued, sought after. The New Bantu Administration was keen on brains from elsewhere. I could also have my place in the regime. I could allow myself to aim high. And Monga Minga, as an army widow, says that to be able to aim high, you have to go into politics. You need to be a card-carrying member of the Democratic Party of Bantuland, the sole party. I could join this party, for example. If I really have to, I will. I will be entirely devoted to it, and I won't miss the opportunity to score my first goal as soon as I enter the field. Monga Minga says that it's the best way of getting noticed. For instance, I'll sing the praises of the military commander of the new administration and his wife. I'll become their disciple. I'll go and evangelise all the lost souls in every corner of Bantuland, even the most remote. I'll go and talk to them in the name of our military commander. I'll win over souls for our national Christian movement. I will have no pity for those who disobey. But first, I'll give them a chance, in the corridors of torture. If they persist, then I'll bury them alive or throw them to the dogs. I'll be promoted. I'll be somebody. I'll be the military commander's right arm. With him, I'll travel all over the place. With him, I'll often return here to our distant cousins' country, on lengthy missions. I'll come back here from time to time, and I won't have a hard time any more. I'll go and donate to the food bank charity. I'll go and visit my adviser at the unemployment office to tell her that I've become somebody. I won't forget Madame Bauer, Monsieur Khalifa, Mireille Laudenbacher and her dog.

Until I can do all that, I must give the best of myself to my internship. My motivation is at rock bottom. The only thing that keeps me there is having to pay my rent. It's the only thing that gives me a reason to get up in the morning. A few weeks ago, I asked Madame Bauer if she could do something for me. Maybe she knew someone who could help me find a little something long term. I'll see, she replied. But I'm not promising anything. And since then, still nothing. Her silence is torture. She's in her world and I'm in mine. She campaigns fiercely on this black sheep issue. Meanwhile, I am living the life of a black sheep. She campaigns for her dear friend Khalifa to be elected in Berne, even though he stands no chance of being elected. He'll remain in Lausanne. Their ideas won't go any further.

16

Mama's illness is a blow to the family, both those who stayed behind in M'fang, from where my mother was driven out for alleged complicity in her husband's murder, and those in M'bangala where she found refuge. In coming to Switzerland, Monga Minga left behind her a host of people for whom naturally she was responsible. Did she not work as a supervisor on a banana plantation? Weren't her two children in Switzerland? It was up to her to take care of her relatives. She also had to take care of those who'd cast her out in M'fang to get their hands on the possessions left by Sangoh. They contacted her again and asked for forgiveness for all the wrongs that their hunger had driven them to commit. Mama welcomed them with open arms. Auntie Botonghi had been against it, from her Geneva place of residence, but Monga Minga had simply reminded her what an important value loyalty is in our society.

In our new home in the M'bangala village, there are still many people eagerly awaiting Monga Minga's return. They're convinced that without her, without my sister and me, they won't be able to cope. There's Ntoumba, for example, the son of Uncle Ezoke's cousin. A strapping twenty-two-year-old. He drags a rickshaw all day long to earn three miserable dry gombos. It's not as if he doesn't have the education to find better. Young Ntoumba has a baccalaureate. But in our country, even more than here in the land of my cousins, unemployment doesn't give a toss about qualifications. So, everyone rolls up their sleeves and gets by as best they can. Since Mama has been ill and can no longer pay his university fees, pulling a rickshaw is how he manages to be self-reliant. He could have gone into the New Bantu Administration's regular army, but he dreams of other things. Apparently, Mama promised to bring him here to Switzerland. Lying in her hospital bed, she often thinks about it. But Kosambela has already told her that there's no room here for Ntoumba. At least, not now. He'll have to wait a little longer.

At home, as well as Ntoumba, there's also Mussango, the nephew of grandmother Ngonda's aunt, who's occupying a little bedroom in the house. There's Nyamsi, my mother's aunt's granddaughter. She sleeps on the living-room floor. There's also Nkempe, Mbendi, Bipoum, Ossolo and loads of others who I don't even know. This host of relatives were all dependent on Monga Minga before misfortune came knocking at her door.

Since Monga Minga has been here, it's my sister Kosambela who takes care of them. She doesn't have a lot of money, but she does what she can. She often asks me if I've got a little gombo to put in the basket. I tell her no. She asks me to pray to Nzambe to make my field of gombo sprout. Since she doesn't have enough either, she appeals to her ex-husband, that thing. At least in situations like this, he can be useful to her. And if he refuses to help, she calls him every name under the sun and even threatens to go and live in Bantuland with her sons. Then her thing of a husband starts to cry and beg her not to take the boys away. He gives in and lets her have everything she asks for.

And so, from time to time, Kosambela helps out the brothers and sisters back home. There are so many mouths to feed that it's never enough to keep everyone afloat. Even less to send Ntoumba to university. Besides, the latest we've heard is that his girlfriend is expecting his baby. In the village, the outraged family are accusing the girl of having stolen this baby from Ntoumba because she knew that Monga Minga was going to send him to Switzerland. They say she's a whore, a witch, a baby-snatcher, a shameless hussy, a bitch. In response, Kosambela simply told Ntoumba that he'd have to keep pulling his rickshaw to pay for his baby's clothes. No way was she going to shower him with gombo when he can't even keep his bangala in his pants for a second.

Kosambela also keeps the family back home informed of Mama's state of health. And that too she does when she can, because on the one hand phone cards for calling home cost a fortune, and on the other, Mama's illness upsets her so much that she doesn't want to talk about it to anyone. Except to the good Lord, maybe.

And so, Kosambela doesn't give them all the news. There's another reason for that. Perhaps one that's much more important than the others. Kosambela says that in our Bantu families, there are too many sorcerers. She says that Bantu sorcery can do harm for no reason. Do harm just for the sake of it, for fun. She says that that kind of sorcery can be lethal. That it kills everything in its path, even corpses. She adds that this black magic knows no borders. And being here, among the Whites, hidden among the snow-capped mountains of Switzerland, thousands of miles from home, doesn't mean that it can't affect us. My sister says that this Bantu sorcery can even make its way across telephone and satellite networks. And so, when she calls the family back in Bantuland, she merely says that everything is fine. She tells them that Mama is doing well, that she'll soon be better, that we simply have to keep believing in miracles. We must keep praying.

'Why don't you tell them the truth?' I asked her this morning when we were in the hospital cafeteria.

She remained composed. Without paying me any visible attention, she carried on eating her apple tart. She left my question hanging in the air. Then she answered calmly.

'*Fratellino*, don't allow yourself to be licked by someone who can swallow you.'

'Ah, there! I was certain. You see evil everywhere. Everywhere!'

'Honestly, all I can do is advise you to pray.'

'Pray for yourself. He who believes in Nzambe knows not fear.'

'May God give you wisdom, *fratellino*.'

'No matter how high you throw something, it always lands back down on the ground.'

'That's what they teach you at the Whites' school. We Bantus believe it can stay up in the air.'

That is Kosambela's crowning argument. She sees the world purely in black and white. She no longer considers me a pure Bantu born and bred. She says I'm too diluted. That I'm a White person with black skin. She insults me, saying I'm a coconut, whereas all I'm asking is that she tells the aunts and uncles in Bantuland the truth. Kosambela maintains her position. That's what she's like – it's very hard to get her to change her opinion. And so, for those left behind in Bantuland, we'll merely say that everything's fine. Everything will be even better by the grace of Nzambe. Period.

In Bantuland, people say: without happiness there can be no sadness. Monga Minga's illness isn't just a bad thing for the entire family and for her. This situation, sad as it is, does however have some plus sides. For example, since Mama's been ill, she's lived here with us in Switzerland. And that is something. I can see her, touch her and talk to her whenever I like. I don't need to travel thousands of kilometres to visit her in the forests of Bantuland. Nor do I need to save up for phone cards to call Africa.

Here, I have a GA, as my Swiss cousins call it. It's an annual travel pass that allows me to take public transport whenever I like and how I like, anywhere in the country. It costs your balls, for sure. But I bought it with the money I earned with Monsieur Nkamba selling beauty products to women and men fed up with the blackness of their skin.

I'd bought a GA with the intention of making it easier to go job-hunting. I didn't want to be hindered by anything. I wanted to be ready to go and work anywhere the possibility arose in Switzerland, even hundreds of kilometres from where I lived. Without that special travel pass, I wouldn't have been able to get to Madame Bauer's offices for my black sheep campaign internship. But the biggest benefit of this pass is undeniably the fact that I can go and see Monga Minga at the other end of Switzerland whenever I want. I simply take the train and cross the entire country, from west to south. I set off from Geneva for Ticino via wherever I like. I drink in the splendid Swiss landscapes: green carpets as far as the eye can see. Mountains that look down on you and command respect. Timid lakes that are silent as the trains pass. Then the inevitable cows! How conceited they are!

Another advantage of Mama's illness is that it has brought Kosambela and me closer. You remember the story of Docta Bernasconi and his marriage to a man. Kosambela had been shocked. When she found out that like Docta Bernasconi, I, her own flesh-and-blood brother whom she loved more than anything, also played for the other team, she fainted.

This whole story came from Auntie Botonghi's lips.

Auntie Botonghi had spotted me holding hands with Ruedi in a narrow back street in Geneva's old town, even though the street wasn't very well lit. That was why I allowed myself the liberty. But something, seemingly insignificant, had given me away: my kongolibon. When my shaven head goes somewhere, it sends reverberations in all directions. So it wasn't very hard for her to think: oh look, that must be Mwana over there. And I don't know what devil had put Auntie Botonghi in that street that evening and at that late hour.

'Hey, my son Mwana! Hello, *Na how na?*'

I recognised Auntie Botonghi's voice at once. I froze. I'd let go of Ruedi's hand to turn around slowly. But too late, she'd already seen everything.

'Um . . . Auntie,' I stuttered.

'I see you're in good company,' she said, darting me one of those mocking smiles that the gossips from our country specialise in.

'Auntie, this is Ruedi.'

They greeted each other. She had dissected Ruedi with her eyes. Then she looked from one to the other of us, nodding her chin and smiling. I felt deeply uncomfortable. What would she go and tell everyone in Bantuland? As for Ruedi, he didn't clock any of this. He simply offered Auntie Botonghi a big smile. His smile was so big that Auntie Botonghi even said at one point:

'You must come and see your auntie one day, my sons, when you have more time. Will you?'

'With pleasure,' Ruedi said.

I'd have given anything to shut him up.

'Right, Auntie, we're in a rush. It's getting late.'

'Have fun, my sons.'

Her 'have fun' said it all. I knew the news would soon spread around the planet. I was done for. I knew Auntie Botonghi very well. My sister and I had lived with her for years. When Kosambela had married her thing of a husband and gone to live with him in his Ticino mountains, I'd stayed at Auntie Botonghi's. I know that her mouth can keep yakking non-stop, morning, afternoon and evening. With some of her friends, who were also my customers, they had tabs on everyone in the French-speaking Black community in Switzerland and even beyond. Until now, I'd been proud that I'd managed to keep details of my private life secret from her. But now my kongolibon had put me in an awkward situation.

Very early the next morning, as I anticipated, my phone rang. It was Monga Minga. At that time, she still had her beautiful, dulcet stage voice.

'Hello! Mwana!'

'Are you well?'

'I'm not calling you about me. I'm calling about you.'

She said this in such an aggressive tone that my only defence was to keep quiet. Then she went on:

'I mean that the situation is serious!'

'What's going on? Is someone back there ill?'

'Leave everyone else out of this. We need to talk, you and me. Because the kind of thing I'm hearing with my ears needs a talk.'

'So talk.'

'Don't hurry me. Let me take my time to find the right words. Because here, we often say that the river takes wrong turns when no one shows it the way.'

'. . .'

'You know very well that since your father's death, I've raised you and your sister all on my own. I've shown you the right path. Nzambe on high is my witness. I fought like a soldier to make you into decent people. I have given everything for you. And I mean everything. I've given everything so that you can live where you live today. What have I not given you, Mwana? You tell me! What have I not given you? What have I not done for you, my son? People even tut-tutted me saying I spoiled you too much. Oh yes! If only I'd known. Too much salt ruins the sauce! What have people not said to me because of you, Mwana?'

'I don't see what you're getting at.'

'You don't see? You don't see that the whole of Bantuland already knows that you're a . . one of *them*?'

'Monga Minga, do you listen to gossip?'

'Isn't it that the ears are made for listening? It may be that people have heard that you were seen in the streets of Geneva lovingly kissing boys. You even do it in the street, in front of everyone?! Not a bit ashamed! Nzambe sees you. My son Mwana, Nzambe sees you! Is it to go and do stupid things with people in the street that I sent you to Geneva?'

'Monga Minga, listen to me . . .'

'. . . No! You're the one who has to listen to me now! You have brought the mother of all shame down on my body!'

Mama had carried on badmouthing me. She'd talked until her phone credits ran out. A few minutes later, she called back. I didn't answer. She tried loads of times. I'd turned off my phone. Then, when I finally answered, a few days later, she said:

'In any case, do as you please. This is your sex life, not mine. Your father up there sees you.'

'Mama . . .'

'Auntie Botonghi told me that . . .'

'. . . So, it's Auntie Botonghi who calls you to tell you nonsense?'

'Who cares about the messenger. It's the message that matters.'

'It's obvious that you've received the message loud and clear.'

'Don't you use your clever White people's French. Drop that when you speak to me. And besides, a little respect please. I'm the one who gave birth to you.'

I did not reply. I let her carry on speaking.

'I was saying that these are your sexual problems. I'm not going to come and poke my nose in. You children of today, when we speak to you, it goes in here and comes out there. Luckily, Auntie Botonghi told me he's a young White boy.'

And the page had been turned. When Mama called me from Bantuland, she also asked after Ruedi. How's our young White boy? she always asked. Sometimes, she even talked to Ruedi on the phone. At first, Ruedi could barely understand Mama's French. They both had their accent and their language. But with time, they'd eventually found common ground.

Although Mama had accepted Ruedi, the same could not be said for Kosambela. Auntie Botonghi had also told her that I was one of *them*. And Kosambela hadn't been able to bring herself to call me as Mama had. When this news reached her ears, she fainted and took a week's sick leave. Yet again, the Manager-Sisters had given it to her.

My sister told herself that all the people she loved ended up falling sick. First of all, her beloved Dottore Bernasconi and now her fratellino. Who next? Her children? Oh no! Not that. Kosambela would sell her soul for her sons not to turn out that way. Also, when she'd learned from Monga Minga's lips that I had gone to the register office with Ruedi, Kosambela had formally banned me from setting foot inside her house. You never know, you might infect my sons, she'd said. Since then, we'd met again at my MA graduation ceremony. Then once more when Mama had sent me food from Bantuland.

But since Mama's been lying in San Salvatore, my sister and I have grown a lot closer. Everything is almost back to normal. She allows me to see my nephews. She asks me if I can babysit them for a night. She even once went so far as to ask me to say hello to Ruedi. That did me a lot of good. And when I told Ruedi himself, he jumped and yelled like a jubilant Alpine boy.

17

My black sheep campaign work placement ended yesterday. Madame Bauer doesn't need me to assist her in her fight any more. She lost the election. She lost in front of the people. She's lost everything. Her foes, on the other hand, the black sheep party, had a landslide win. They even gained new seats in the federal parliament and strengthened their lead as the country's main political party.

Yesterday, when I left the office for the last time, I left behind a defeated, vexed Madame Bauer. This time, she'd given it her all. Her all. And she clung on. Her victory would have been a golden trophy to crown all the battles that have marked her career as a lifelong activist. She never stops talking about her fears for the future of our society. Now we have a parliament of black sheep, she states, offended, trying somehow to keep her anger simmering. She broods on her anxiety. She mutters her pessimism. Over and over again, she repeats her inability to understand to anyone who'll listen – in other words me. Only me, because no journalists are interested in Madame Bauer any longer.

The night the results were announced, at the end of October, the last mikes recorded her opinion. They also picked up her tears of disappointment. The journalists, a handful of admirers, politicians of all stripes, including from the NLM, comforted her. Here, after an election or a referendum, some always claim with bitter pride that the results of the ballot box aren't that important. They say that the main thing for them is the debate the issue sparked beforehand. Madame Bauer has no wish to burden herself with this consolation prize. She was conscious of her failure. And others made it even clearer, by asking a poisonous question or making a barbed comment. Then they again paid tribute to her persistence, her determination to fight relentlessly for so many years. They were aware that all this was coming to an end. It couldn't be otherwise after so many consecutive defeats. Perhaps she would soon retire. Probably. And if she didn't have the grace to step down herself, she would simply be pushed out. That's why they paid tribute to her contribution.

Then the mikes disappeared. Requests for interviews and comments too. Her press releases now go straight into the waste-paper bins of those journalists from the new generation who are so much in demand. For the past month, Madame Bauer has been consigned to oblivion, to the archive, until the next event that may mean that people still remember her. But when will that be? She must wait. And she will wait alone, because even Mireille Laudenbacher has pulled out of the race. She decided to leave, after all those years of collaboration. Now she's going to work full-time for an animal rights association.

Even her dear friend Khalifa has made himself increasingly scarce. He must have withdrawn to digest his latest defeat in silence. This time, he has missed out on being a member of the national parliament. He'll be left defending his ideals in the Vaud wilderness where there will be only his own ears to hear him. Since the results of the elections, his party has disintegrated, dispersed. It no longer has a head or a tail. A violent and spectacular explosion that the journalists take a perverse delight in writing about. Khalifa knows very well that he will be alone in living with the impression that he never knew how to woo the voters, that he had not been charming enough. He'll be alone in coping with his failure like his dear friend Madame Bauer, whom I said goodbye to yesterday at the association's headquarters.

As for me, I feel sorry for all these good people. But I'm not sorry that it's all over now. At any rate, I wasn't doing much there since the announcement of the results. And I had other things on my mind. One more day there and I'd have dropped dead. I'm glad all that has come to an end.

The downside is that I'm going to have to go back to the unemployment office. I'll see that waiting room again, the people sitting there in silence-patience-distance mode. I'm going to see the unemployment lady again, with her three hairs playing leapfrog on top of her head. Who knows, I might even see the guy who smashed the mirror in the lift, or hell, I might even do the same. When I think about all that, I feel a knot in my stomach. And why go back to the unemployment office? In any case, they won't be able to do anything for me. The adviser lady told me so a thousand times. I still haven't paid enough contributions. You need at least a year's salary over the past two years. Which I don't have. I've only done a brief three-month internship. That's not enough for me to qualify for unemployment benefit. And without that benefit, I'm not entitled to any other support to help me find work.

Oh! One piece of good news: I received a job offer last week. I'd forgotten all about it. I'd replied to an ad. I sent my application for a laugh. But I'd been selected. I'll be the African dance instructor for employees of an international NGO. Apparently, it will be good for the employees and make them more efficient. Especially in winter.

Once a week, my job will be to make them raise their legs to their necks, wiggle their bums, jump up and touch the clouds, clap their hands or yell like idiots. All that to the sound of a balafon or a frenzied mvet. It will be called: African dance class. They'll pay me a tiny something, of course. But oh, what a surprise when they asked me to work illicitly. It's easier, isn't it? said the HR gentleman I spoke to on the phone. He said it with a smile that I could hear very well. I remembered that I'm not entitled to unemployment benefit today even though I've worked for a number of years . . . I said no. He pressed me. I negotiated. He agreed to pay my health insurance contributions for a reduced salary. *Cioè.*

We still rely on the food bank to eat. But what are we to do about the other expenses?

'We'll have to go and see the social security people,' I said to Ruedi this morning.

'Are you kidding? Can you see me going to social security?'

'If we've been to the food bank, we can go to social security too.'

A silence gives way to reflection.

'Otherwise, you let your parents help us out.'

'We're not going to live off them.'

'At any rate, with or without their help, we're going to social security.'

'Mwana! Social security is humiliating. You've been living here long enough, don't you realise?'

'And being unemployed? And being hounded for non-payment of bills? And working without being able to feed ourselves? Isn't that humiliating?'

Ruedi hangs his head. And because he says nothing, I seize the opportunity to bring it up again:

'I'm doing everything that's humanly possible to find a solution, and monsieur here is doing fuck all to help me. And you talk to me about humiliation. What do *you* know about humiliation? You are from a good family. Have you ever gone without food? Have you ever suffered? *Social security is humiliating* . . . *social security is humiliating* . . . What are you doing to avoid us having to go there? Tell me!'

Ruedi says nothing. I'm not surprised. He doesn't like arguments, as I still remember very clearly at the start of our relationship. The way we met was classic: a cute little redhead steps on my Louboutins in a club. I yell as if my toe's been torn out. I yell more for my shoes than for my foot. Shit, they cost me a fortune! The cute redhead apologises. I insult him as I would have done in Bantuland when I was still under my father's military protection. He turns red. He apologises again. He's a bit wasted. His voice grows even softer. He tries to support my shoulder. Let go of me, you idiot! I say. He finds a seat in a corner and sits there silently. I watch him from where I'm wiping off my shoes. His friends come to his rescue. He politely asks them to leave him alone. He remains on his own. At one point, he gets up and heads for the exit. Then I realise that I was probably too harsh on him. I follow him out. I catch up with him. Shyly, I apologise. Still, I tell him never to make the mistake of dirtying my lovingly polished shoes again. Hey, these are Louboutins! We laugh. He tells me he's nineteen. I'm twenty-four. We have a ciggy. Then another. We talk about clothes. Then we end up in my uni studio flat. He's not so bad. He quickly becomes a sort of fuck-buddy for when my balls are bursting. A spare wheel. Months and seasons go by. I note that his name is Ruedi. Ruedi Baumgartner, the sort of name that the Bantu I am will have trouble remembering. I see him a few times. Then regularly. We become friends. We become lovers. Without really thinking about it, we decide to move in together to the little apartment we still live in now. In the meantime, a law allows couples like ours to enter into a civil partnership. We take advantage of it to do so, more as an experiment than out of conviction. I work for Nkamba African Beauty. He's a student. Everything is going well. Very well, even. Then I lose my job, my mother falls seriously ill, and the hassles begin.

'We don't need to go to social security. You're going to start giving dance lessons soon and we'll cope.'

'You make me laugh. The dance classes won't even pay our rent.'

'So you can dance in the street too and busk.'

His suggestion makes me laugh. Ruedi has never been able to raise his voice to me. But he's often hit the right note with a joke and deflated me. I can't help laughing. It's one of the rare things we manage to do every so often. When things are bad, we laugh. When I receive a reminder or a final warning to pay a bill which I know I'll never be able to pay, we laugh. When we have bellyache or we're constipated from stuffing ourselves with lentils, we laugh. When we have to put on shirts, trousers, socks or underpants that are old and full of holes, we laugh.

But alone, all alone, when Ruedi's at university and I'm on my own at home, I cry.

18

This morning, Ruedi and I are defying the snowstorm that's brought the entire city to a standstill. We're going to the social security office. Ruedi will do the talking. We reckon they'll find him more credible.

We're received by a Black guy. We're delighted. Maybe he'll make things easier for us. We have to walk down a long corridor to his office. Close to his chair is a small wooden statue. It's a Bantu carving – I can tell from the details. On the desk, a prominently displayed photo shows him with a pretty white woman and a little mixed-race child who must be his daughter, she looks so much like him. Next to this family portrait, a nameplate shows: Mazongo Mabeka. It's the same as the one on the door of the office where we're sitting now. With a name like that, it would be very unlikely that this social worker was not from Bantuland. I'm certain of that.

Monsieur Mazongo Mabeka asks a lot of questions which Ruedi answers without much difficulty and with tact. Why are we there? How did we get to this point? What are our jobs? What about our families? Ruedi lies. He says his parents haven't given him anything since he started living with me. I simply reply to the questions that are only about me. Where do I come from? Why and how did I come to be in Switzerland? I tell Monsieur Mazongo Mabeka everything. He doesn't bat an eyelid. He's ultra-serious. Why can't I find work? I explain all my efforts to do so and he darts me a look that suggests I should try harder. That surprises me. He's Bantu, he must understand what it's like for me. I smile all the same. I know why I'm here. I absolutely don't tell him that soon I'm going to be giving African dance classes. He'll reduce our benefits.

Once the interview is over, Ruedi and I smile at the thought of receiving our gombo allowance to improve our day-to-day lives. Monsieur Mazongo Mabeka consults his computer like a marabout his talismans. I take advantage of the silence to try and find out more about Monsieur Mazongo Mabeka's roots.

'Excuse me, Monsieur Mazongo Mabeka . . .' I say.

'Yes?'

'Are you from Bantuland?'

'No.' He smiles. 'I am Swiss.'

'But where are you from originally?' asks Ruedi.

'I have just told you that I'm Swiss.'

'OK.'

'Any other questions?'

'No,' I say.

Monsieur Mazongo Mabeka continues to work at his computer. When he's finished, he holds out a sheet of paper with a list of all the documents we need to bring. Once we've submitted all these documents, the social security verification department will have to confirm their authenticity. Then a committee will decide on the merits of our application. And then, and only then, may we perhaps be entitled to social security benefits.

Ruedi and I are disappointed not to be able to receive any money right away. How long will it take before our benefits come through? Monsieur Mazongo Mabeka tells us he doesn't know. He says he'll make a report, then the committee will decide. He tells us that most importantly it will all depend on the speed with which we bring the requisite documents. The sooner we do that, the sooner we can receive help, he says. Ruedi and I glance at the list of documents we have to bring. A long series of papers: ID card, rental agreement, health insurance policy, family record book, and copies of the past twelve months' bank statements . . .

'And how much can we hope to receive?' Ruedi shoots back.

'I can't tell you for now,' replies Monsieur Mazongo Mabeka. 'First of all, the committee has to meet and then decide on the amount you will be allocated.'

'But it's possible to give a rough idea,' Ruedi presses him.

'Let's say around fifteen hundred francs.'

'What?! But that doesn't even cover our rent!'

'Monsieur Baumgartner, we don't usually help students. If a student needs help, they can apply for a grant. We are making an exception for you because you and your partner are a couple.'

'Talk, monsieur. It's all talk!'

'But that's the law.'

'And I'm talking to you about realities. You, who are so Swiss, do you think we can live on fifteen hundred francs a month?'

'Monsieur Baumgartner . . .'

'Crap.'

'Monsieur Baumgartner, please mind your language.'

'You talk to me about the law. *That's the law, that's the law.* What do you understand of our life? What do you understand of what we're going through? You live your nice life, and you talk to me about the law?'

It's the first time I've seen Ruedi in such a state. I have to stop this argument. If Monsieur Mazongo Mabeka puts a spoke in our wheel, we'll never get out of this mess, and no one will help us. I immediately defuse the situation.

'We'll bring you the documents you have asked for as soon as possible,' I say.

'Thank you, Monsieur Matatizo.'

I drag Ruedi towards the door. He's red with anger. And when a redhead turns red with anger, it's not always pretty-pretty. So I do my utmost to get him to calm him down and return to normal, like the Ruedi who I'm used to seeing, my Ruedi. But no, he's still red and angry. When we leave the social worker's office, Ruedi vents all the swear words he has in him. And, wait for it, he yells them in Schweizerdeutsch, like a volley of machine-gun fire. I speak to him in French to save him from hurting his lips with his Schweizerdeutsch. He wants to go in the lift, but I suggest we take the stairs. Because I'm afraid there might be a mirror in the lift. And who knows?

Ruedi might smash it, he's so mad. He's even angrier to see the list of documents we have to bring to be entitled to benefits. We have to give them everything. Everything. We have to drop our pants to get emergency support. What shocks Ruedi most is that we're being asked for copies of all our bank transactions over the past twelve months. For a true-true Eidgenosse in his primeval state like Ruedi, nosing around in his bank account, even if there's nothing in it, is like cutting off his balls. He's absolutely incensed at this demand.

Once we're outside the social security building, Ruedi can't stop railing against the system, the laws, Monsieur Mazongo Mabeka and so on and so on. His insults rain down as thick as the snowstorm. At one point, he bursts into tears. *Scheisse! Scheisse! Scheisse!* Why is our life such hell when we haven't done anyone any harm? Why? Eh! We've been in this shit for months and there's no one to help us. Your unemployment people tell you to get lost. The bastards! And anyway, why should you even be unemployed? Why!? You have a good degree. You're no fool, are you? You're bright and you have a lot of skills. But none of them will give you a job. That's right, none of them. And why is that, do you think?! You act as if you can't see what's going on. Are you blinkered or what? Are you blind? You refuse to face up to the facts. With all your qualifications, you're going to give stupid African dance classes for shitty pay, whereas your friends are living the good life in executive jobs. *Scheisse! Scheisse!*

'What is this fucking world? *Scheisse!* Crap! Do you hear me? *Scheisse!* Me, despite everything, despite my family and everything, I'm reliant on the food bank. We depend on the food bank like miserable beggars. And if it weren't for that, we'd already be dead. We are dead. We're already dead. Dead and buried. D'you hear me? These are our remains. And did you hear that idiot earlier? An arsehole! An imbecile! An upstart! I am Swiss. I am Swiss . . . I am Swiss. NLM-African! Swiss *Scheisse*! Swiss, my arse! *Huereverdammte Schiissdräck! Gottverdammte Seich!*

He wants to yell more, but I put my arms around him. He struggles violently. Then weakly. But I overpower him. Easily. I put my arms around him and stroke his head, the back of his neck, his back, for ages. My Ruedi. Everything will be all right. Calm down. You'll see. We'll get through this. With or without the laws, it'll be all right. With or without Monsieur Mazongo Mabeka, it'll be all right. Calm down. Calm down now. Let's go home. Let's not stay here. Come with me. Let's get out of here.

19

It's become a routine. I go to Lugano every Friday, and I come back to Geneva on Sunday evening. The train journeys are long and tiring. At least six hours each way. That's almost as many hours as it takes to fly to Bantuland . . . But you end up getting used to it. On the train, I either read or make do with African comedies. I know that Monga Minga loves African comedies, especially those from West Africa. So, when I get to the hospital, I fill her ears with them. She laughs. But recently, her laughter has only been a thin laugh and I am the only person who sees it. Since they've been injecting her with chemo, she's been transformed. Her face is so distorted, puffy, dark, that it's hard to decipher the faintest expression.

'How are we doing, Monga Minga?' I ask, walking into Mama's room.

She doesn't turn around. She's facing towards the bay window. She must be gazing at the snow. She still hasn't had the opportunity to touch the white gold from the sky that many Bantus dream of seeing at least once in their lifetimes. She must content herself with feasting her eyes on it. Her hospital room has become a prison. Docta Bernasconi and his team have put her on high alert. They say her antibodies have fallen so low that the slightest contact with the slightest germ could be fatal. So, to visit Mama, first of all you have to sanitise your hands. Then you have to put on the paraphernalia that's just outside the door of her room. It's like a surgeon's outfit: white gloves, a green mask, an orange skullcap that must cover all your hair, a not-very-elegant yellow smock, and disposable blue overshoes.

This get-up is a double ordeal: first of all, the mix of colours is just horrible, and secondly, I lose any real contact with Mama. Those gloves, the mask, the toga-smock and all the rest are a barrier to touching. It feels as if I'm seeing her through a glass wall. The first time I had to put on all the clobber, I cried for ages before going into the room. I felt as if Mama was moving one step further away from me. I felt as if day after day she was finding ways of getting away from us, from my sister and me. She was distancing herself. She was departing.

'How are we doing, Monga Minga?' I ask again.

Mama lies still, her face still turned towards the bay window. Something seems wrong. I feel my heart begin to race. What's the matter with her? Why isn't she moving? Perhaps she's fallen asleep. Yes, that must be it. She can only be asleep. Otherwise, why wouldn't she want to answer me? Or at least turn to greet me with her eyes?

I tiptoe over to her as if afraid of the discovery I am about to make. I place my hand on her shoulder, murmuring: my little lady. She turns slowly, painfully, towards me. I give a sigh of relief. You gave me a fright,

I tell her. My heart doesn't have a chance to calm down before I am already concerned about something else. Mama is crying. Why are you crying? I ask her. Nothing, she whispers.

I really don't like that kind of answer. At any other time, I would have told her so. But now, I calm myself. I pull a chair towards me. I sit down and take Mama's hand in mine. Don't cry. Please don't cry. She snivels all the more, like a child demanding its mother. Tell me everything. What's the matter? Are you in pain? Tummyache? Your throat? She says nothing. She just cries. Whatever's the matter with you? Then I give up asking and simply carry on stroking her hand.

'This illness is killing me,' she manages to murmur. She struggles to get the words out, between gasps. 'Look at me. Look at me, Mwana, my son. Do you still recognise me? Look what this illness has done to me. It's stolen my beauty, my hair, my face, my femininity. It's stolen everything from me in such a short time. Look at me, my son. Look how I've aged. What can I have done to Nzambe to deserve this? What harm have I done? I am not rich. Cancer, my son, I have always been told is a disease of the White people. But am *I* rich? Why me? Why this? Why?'

I cry. It's the first time that Mama has actually said anything about what's happening to her. She's always had the strength to make light of this battle. She's always managed to find the words to make anyone who visits her laugh. Even the San Salvatore hospital staff admire her fighting spirit. But now, the burden is becoming heavier and heavier to bear. How can a person remain like this, imprisoned in a hospital room, when they've had a life like Mama's? How can they lie there all day waiting for their morphine injections? Having been a public actress in the New Bantu Administration theatre company? Having married an army man from our country? Having shared her husband with her best friend? Having lost her husband and seen her in-laws rush in to grab her possessions and throw her into the street? Having fought tooth and nail to succeed? How can a person accept such a precarious situation when they've experienced all that?

I cry and I put my arms around Mama. We both cry. The pain is so intense that I feel cramps gnawing my stomach. I sing Mama a hymn. She falls asleep. I stay beside her, gazing at her dramatically changed face. I cry again. It's so hard to recognise Mama. I get a grip on myself, saying it is better to have my mama in this condition and alive than to have her with all her beauty dead and buried.

We're roused by a nurse. I had fallen asleep at Mama's feet. The nurse has come to give Mama her morphine. When she's done, I go out onto the balcony. I make a snowball and bring it in to Mama. She smiles at me. She touches the snow. She looks happy.

20

Mama complains about the nurses. She tells me she hasn't washed all day. That she tried to ask the good ladies if they would take her to the washroom for a shower. She says that those ladies didn't pay her the slightest attention. That their attitude is uncaring. Probably because she is there out of charity, she thinks. She talks, talks and talks. She says all the bad things she thinks about the nurses looking after her. She even says that she doesn't want to stay in this hospital any longer.

Silence. I don't know how to reply to Mama's grievances. I want to go and see the nurses to have a word with them, so I stand up and head towards the door. Then I stop. What if Mama was exaggerating again? If that was not actually how things were? And besides, how does Mama make herself understood by the nurses? She doesn't speak a word of Italian. Neither do I. How would I be able to go and speak to them?

I retrace my steps.

I sit down on the bed, beside Mama. I take her hand back in mine.

'Aren't you going to talk to them?' she asks.

I don't answer straightaway. I simply stroke her hand. She calms down. Silence reigns again. There's too much light in the room. A bright sun is shining outside after the snow that's been falling these past few days. I gaze absently at Mama's kongolibon. She has such a beautiful head that I wonder why she's never chosen to have a shaved head before.

I tell Mama that it isn't easy to get over the language barrier between her and her nurses. No and no. She protests. She says that all the same, this is Switzerland. And reminds me that in this country, people speak several languages.

'I'm not asking them to speak French-French. Anyway, I myself don't speak that kind of French. But . . . a shower? A patient who asks to have a shower, it's not exactly Chinese, is it?'

Mama says it's like that all the time. She never gets to have her shower. At least, not first-first thing in the morning, as she would like. In our country, a self-respecting woman has her shower and washes her private parts early in the morning, as soon as she wakes up. Here, they always ask her to wait. She has to wait because she's not the only patient on that floor and the nurses have to deal with more urgent cases: a patient who's fallen out of bed and is bleeding profusely, a patient having a fit, and so on. Here, she often has to wait until ten, eleven, even twelve o'clock. She says she doesn't want to wait any more. She says that even when they give her the shower, they don't let the water run down below.

'What kind of woman doesn't shower down below?'

In her description of her woes, Mama ramps up to the next level – threats. She says that if those nurses don't come early in the morning to take her for her shower, then she'll go on her own. I can't help bursting out laughing as I listen to Mama's threat. Where will she get the strength to get out of bed unaided to go and have her shower?

I give her a foot massage. Her feet are swollen, limp, with no movement any more. It is such a long time since she's stood on her two feet. She's always lying down or buckled into a wheelchair, under supervision. She hasn't been steady on her feet for weeks and weeks.

'It would be really brilliant if you went and had your shower on your own,' I say, laughing.

She scowls, then can't help smiling at me. She laughs.

'You are a naughty boy, my son Mwana. A very naughty boy.'

When I come and visit her, I talk about everything and nothing. I tell her about my long days of job-hunting. I tell her about those international officials who have rigid bodies. Sticks of wood. I tell her all the stories of my recent work placement campaigning against the black sheep. I tell her about Madame Bauer, a lifelong smoker but who's never had any health problems. I describe Mireille Laudenbacher who continues to pay tens of thousands of Swiss francs to save her dog from being put down. I also talk to her about my darling Ruedi. About Monsieur Mazongo Mabeka to whom we eventually sent all the requisite documents so that we'd be entitled to benefits. I go back to my childhood memories under the military protection of Papa, whose ear she bit because he was beating Kosambela. I talk to her about Auntie Botonghi who spends her time poking her nose into people's business in Geneva.

When I tell her all this, we laugh. It does us good. But it also hurts her, in her stomach, where they had inserted a tube to feed her, because her mouth was no longer any use. It hurts, but we laugh anyway. We laugh till we cry. It's as if all is well. Then, she starts coughing again. She coughs hard. She's choking. Phlegm. A lot of phlegm in the little disposable kidney dish. Blood-streaked sputum. Faintness. A pinch of shame, probably. Heart pounding. Giddiness. Unease. Her throat. Pain. Painful throat. All this shit sobers us. No laughing here. You mustn't laugh here. Here, there is sickness. Here, there is disease. Here, people are sad.

21

Ruedi and I receive a letter in the post from Monsieur Mazongo Mabeka informing us that our benefits application has been successful. We will receive two thousand five hundred francs in total, in other words, a thousand francs more than his estimate. On top of that, they'll pay for my health insurance.

That is very good news. Ruedi has agreed to talk to his family, and I've just now received the gombo from social security. It's freshly in my bank account. In addition to this income, there's what I earn from my African dance classes. Our situation is improving. It's such a long time since I saw so much money. No more food bank. No more lentils. No more suffering. At last, we'll be able to try and live like everyone else. I even plan to buy myself a new pair of shoes soon. I'll get myself some Louboutins this afternoon. Since that time when I first met Ruedi, I haven't bought any.

In the kitchen, I put on some music, the current hit 'No one' by Alicia Keys. I sing along at the top of my voice: she's right – everything *is* gonna be all right! I dance all my joy at seeing this change in our situation. I'd have liked to celebrate with Ruedi, but the boy hadn't slept at home last night. He'd been at

Dominique's, in Carouge. Dominique! It's ages since I've seen that guy! He'd promised me a fillet of beef. I tell myself that I'll have to make some time to go see him and eat his meat.

There's another letter on the kitchen table. I open it. It's another rejection letter. I don't give a shit. No more stress. At least for a good while. I carry on dancing until my phone rings and interrupts me. It's Madame Bauer on the line. She's shouting. She sounds very excited. Behind her, I can make out the voices of Mireille Laudenbacher and her friend Khalifa. I didn't think they were together any more. Madame Bauer is yelling with excitement. I yell with excitement too.

'He's gone!' says Madame Bauer. 'It's over. He's gone.'

I turn off my music to concentrate on the call with Madame Bauer. I realise that we are not excited about the same thing. Who is she talking about?

'He's been ousted! He hasn't been re-elected to the government!' gloats Madame Bauer.

'Um . . . Great! Um . . . who exactly has been ousted?'

Madame Bauer tells me that the party leader, the one the media always say has loads of gombo, hasn't been re-elected to the government. It's a spectacular twist! Here, in my cousins' country, the government is entirely elected, or re-elected by the parliament after the general election. The party that wins the general election can expect easily to elect or re-elect its candidates for the government made up of seven ministers. Well, no. The father of the black sheep has not been re-elected, and Madame Bauer is utterly delighted. She asks me to drop by their office.

They're holding an impromptu drinks party to celebrate this wonderful news.

I think about the Louboutins I want to buy that afternoon and I tell myself I'd better decline her invitation. But as I'm about to make up some excuse to avoid their anti-black sheep drinks, Madame Bauer informs me that Mireille Laudenbacher has a very important piece of news for me. She'd like to introduce me to someone who could help me in my job search.

Mireille Laudenbacher comes to the phone. 'Hello, Mwana. How are you?'

'Fine, fine.'

'We're very happy, as you can hear.'

She goes on about the ousting of their sworn enemy. I smile at her. I tell her how delighted I too am at this development. I'm expecting her to mention the man she wants to introduce me to. But she's taking her time. Then she gets going.

'Monsieur Burioni! I've already made an appointment for you with him and you absolutely have to be there. On the seventeenth of December. Madame Bauer and I are truly very happy to have worked with you. So, when Monsieur Burioni told me he needed someone for his new business, I immediately thought of you. I said to myself that you'd be ideal. Monsieur Burioni needs people like you.'

'Oh, thank you very much, Mireille! I'm really delighted.'

'You're welcome. You're a good boy. And besides, you'll see, omigod, omigod, how well Burioni pays. You'll be treated royally! I'm convinced he'll take you on. But you do have to go to an interview on the seventeenth of December.'

'And what's the job?'

'Oh, the work you'll be doing! Won-der-ful! Monsieur Burioni is one of my closest friends, you know. He's helped me a great deal. My dog isn't going to be put down, and it's thanks to him. He's a very good lawyer. He's opening an animal rights law firm in Lausanne. He'll represent animals. And he needs someone like you to do the admin, marketing and communications.'

'Great!'

'Great, great, Mwana!'

Madame Bauer takes back the phone. 'Mwana, aren't you coming to celebrate with us?'

'Yes, yes, I'll jump on the next train.'

22

The day of my interview. Zürich station is heaving. A huge Christmas market has been set up on the concourse. Aromas of mulled wine and toffee waft from the chalet-type stalls and hover over the entire station. Passengers come and go, sucked into the fairground ambiance. As for me, I keep my head down; I find the music and the glaring lights aggressive. My eyes are stinging from the cold. It's snowing. I look at the young soldiers muffled in their army uniforms, their guns on their shoulders. One of them jostled me. I don't think he realised. Otherwise, he'd have apologised. I keep going. My train leaves in five minutes. Anyhow, I don't have the time or the inclination to look at all that's going on around me. My heart is heavy. I want only one thing: to sit down somewhere in the warm and process everything that's happened to me during the past few hours.

In Lugano, I left Mama in a critical condition. I left behind me a weak, listless mother. My mother is crushed. I don't know whether I'll see her again next week. I think I should have stayed. My presence would most likely have done her a lot of good. But she was the one who asked me to go. She told me with a feeble movement of her finger. A tiny, mysterious gesture, insignificant incomprehensible even. But a gesture that I eventually deciphered. During the last three days that I'd spent with her, that had been our only means of communication. She and I were the only ones who understood the code. Not even Kosambela, who came in during her break, was able to grasp anything. Of course, I did what I could, because it wasn't easy, not for me, but even less for her. But I think I'd decoded more or less everything. I think I understood everything she asked me to do: stay, come closer, don't leave me, hug me, stay here . . . that was the main substance of our communication. Stay. Come closer. Don't leave me. Hug me. Stay here. And . . . perhaps too a 'go on, off you go!' I'm certain she was very happy to know that at last I'd got a job interview. Otherwise, she wouldn't have asked me to leave. She'd have kept me beside her, maybe until the end.

This weekend, Mama was completely silent. Silent as a grave.

It's already a few days or even a few weeks since she stopped speaking properly. She just whispers. A little murmur that allows us to keep hoping. She whispers, or we have to pay close attention to her lips which she tries to move slowly, painfully. Her mouth and lips are covered in bleeding sores. And that blood-red carpet doesn't only cover her oral cavity. It unfurls down to her throat and further, throughout her entire digestive system. It goes to the end, as Docta Bernasconi explained to my sister. Apart from her mouth, Mama's eyes are closed the whole time. Feebly, when she tries to open them, she manages it. I thank Nzambe and my ancestors for this feat. But for how many seconds? During this tiny window of time, you can only half-see her black pupils. Then it's the whites that show. Then a bit of both. Then she closes them again. You can't see any more. You have the impression that she is taken hostage by the disease consuming her.

A catheter connected to an implantable port, a sort of gruesome leech attached to her right shoulder, pours a liquid into her at regular intervals. She submits. She has no choice. Docta Bernasconi says it's for her own good. She's just lying there. Knocked out. Diminished. She's a limp vegetable. Too limp. Incapable of the slightest movement except for that forefinger which she activates. It's a skeleton service.

A team of nurses take turns at Mama's bedside. There's a night shift that comes on duty just before or after the Manager-Sisters' evening prayers. They watch over Mama's inert body. They pour countless chemicals into her. During the night, it's the same dance. Each one comes and injects a chemical into her. Then morning comes, and the night shift must leave her in a good state before going off and placing her in the hands of a fresh team. The nurses remove everything that she's expelled during the night. They do as they would with an infant. They also wash her. I don't know whether they pour water down below as she demanded so insistently when she still had the strength to say what she wanted. Kosambela told me recently that they can't really pour water down below because it's just a mass of sores. After leaving Mama properly taken care of, walled up in her silence, they bid me goodbye, ciao.

The new team of nurses arrives. Very often they are smiling, often tired, as if they've been sitting up all night like me. Two or three of them are simply insipid. With no substance. Their 'buongiorno' is tinged with the winter cold. I can even sometimes see in their eyes that they don't really give a shit. Apparently, the most important thing for them is all the stuff they have to pour into Mama's body. I don't know what they're injecting into her. Nor do I want to enquire. I've often asked Kosambela, but she has no idea either. It's too complicated for her. All she tells me is to keep praying that Nzambe, Elolombi and the Bankoko will hear us. Anyway, knowing what they're giving Mama won't make any difference to my fears. Before, I found it hard to see all that, but with time, it's become a routine. I simply look helplessly at the claw they've attached to her right shoulder, beneath her flesh.

Yesterday, Clara was the nurse watching Mama. I'm always very pleased when Clara is in charge. For one thing, she speaks French. With a heavy Milanese accent, for sure, but at least she speaks it. I've always had the feeling that she takes better care of Mama. She smiles a lot, she's very attentive and there's a lot of gentleness in her movements. Even when she gives Mama an injection, I have the impression that she does it with a great deal of affection. Mama said so too, when she could still speak. Since she's stopped talking, Clara is one of the only nurses who continues to talk to her, ask her questions. Even if Mama doesn't reply, Clara still talks to her. She asks her if she's slept well. She asks her if she'd like a little piece of chocolate, even though she's well aware that Mama can't swallow anything. But she asks anyway, and with a big smile. The kind of smile that makes you forget your sorrows. A rare smile. Clara alone smiles like that. Kosambela once told me that she was the only one to pour water down below when Mama wanted it. That's why Mama loves her too.

One time, I asked Clara why she was so kind to Mama. She replied that she was kind to all the patients. Then she admitted that she was especially fond of Mama. She told me that a few years ago her own mother had died from this same type of cancer. As she told me this, her eyes filled with tears. I was deeply sorry for her. But she reassured me: just because my mother died from it, it doesn't mean that yours will die too. Nowadays, science has made a great deal of progress, she went on, and everything is possible. You must have faith.

The train has just started moving. Facing me are two young men dressed up as Santas. They smile at me. I don't know why, but their smile makes me harden my expression. I prefer to cling to my memories of the past hours. I picture Mama as I left her: her face all puffy, darkened, greatly darkened, her red lips on which they keep putting loads of balm to try and stop the bleeding. Lying there, her head turned to one side, her mouth falls open and a trickle of red saliva runs out. Delicately, I dab it away with a handkerchief. Yesterday, her eyes watered. When I wiped her tears, they too were red. Blood oozing out everywhere. Clara was even more present in Mama's room this weekend. She came almost every hour. She kept a very close eye on how the situation was developing. She also injected Mama with morphine. I thought it was morphine anyway, and Kosambela later told me that I was right.

Clara came in to give another injection. She looked at the machine next to Mama. Then she tensed up. She stopped smiling and pressed the fluorescent button by the door of Mama's room. The button changed from green to red. Then, she abruptly asked me to leave the room. I was holding Mama's hand and had no intention of slipping away like that. Mwana, you have to leave now, she said. I wanted to ask her what was going on, but a cohort of nurses had already arrived. I panicked. Monga Minga! I shouted, holding her communication forefinger. She remained inert. Silent, cold, peaceful. Calm. A nurse led me out of the room, gently but firmly.

Once in the corridor, I wanted to scream. Maybe to cry. But I couldn't. I took out my phone to inform Kosambela. She was working all weekend, but I still tried. Her phone was off. Voice message. She must be busy cleaning the room of another patient dying in another part of the hospital. I was distracted for a moment, thinking of everything they might be doing to Mama's body at that moment. To drive those images from my mind, I thought of phoning Ruedi. He won't pick up, I told myself. He's with Dominique again. I tried anyway, and as expected, he hadn't taken his phone with him. And even if he had picked up, he probably wouldn't have grasped the seriousness of what was happening. And if he had understood the seriousness, he still wouldn't have been able to breathe life back into my mother. Who could I call now? Who can come to my aid? I felt so weak. I fell to my knees. I caught myself praying. I invoked Nzambe, Elolombi and my ancestors, the Bankoko. I invoked my father. Pa!!! Pa . . . pa . . . pa . . . paaa!!! I called, trembling feverishly. Papa, where are you? Don't take Monga Minga from us, I beg you. Don't leave us all alone. Do you hear me, Papa? Tell me you won't take Mama. Tell me that she'll stay with us. I've found work. She must enjoy its fruits. Papa!!! Tell me that you're listening to me!

I clutched my stomach which suddenly hurt.

A nurse walked past me. She was with a gentleman. They quickened their pace before stopping in front of the protective equipment they had to put on before going into Mama's room. He must be a doctor, I thought. It's not Bernasconi. But my sister had told me that in Bernasconi's absence, there are always one or two doctors to take over. Their stethoscopes around their necks, they put on gloves and the other gear and dashed into Mama's room. Outside, I waited. Waited. Waited for some news to filter from that room where there were now some ten nurses and a doctor. I waited for someone to tell me that there was still hope. I waited for someone to tell me that Monga Minga was having us on, that it was a trick, that she was play-acting. I waited for around thirty minutes in total. Endless. Then the doctor came out, accompanied by two nurses. They looked tired. The battle they'd just waged seemed to have exhausted them. The gentleman came up to me and said:

'Claudio Schwarz. I'm looking after your mother while Doctor Bernasconi is away.' He also spoke French.

'How is she?'

'Everything is under control.'

'Thanks be to Nzambe!' I yell.

'We've done our utmost.'

I rushed into Mama's room. She lay there, eyes closed, her face even puffier, the skin on her head bare and wrinkled. I went closer. A nurse handed me a mask and gloves to remind me of the regulations. I put them on. I took Mama's hand. I looked at her right forefinger. She waggled it up and down. She must be trying to tell me that she was feeling better. That she'd come through this. Or not. What do I know?

In the packed train, as I go over everything in my mind, I cry. My neighbours dressed up as Santas notice. They are visibly uncomfortable. The look in their eyes shows their lack of understanding. How can a person be crying so near to Christmas? They glance at me again. Trying to show sympathy.

I carry on crying. I do my best not to sob noisily. But the grief gnawing at my insides is too strong. I blow my nose noisily. I cover my head with my jacket hood. I don't want to alert the entire compartment.

After a few long minutes of tears, I manage to doze off. I haven't slept for two nights. Mama's condition kept me vigilant.

Then, like in a dream, I feel a hand on my shoulder. It's pressing me. No, I'm not dreaming. There is indeed someone who's trying to waken me. Slowly, I raise my hood. The glaring light hurts my eyes. I put a hand over my face for protection. I don't have time to emerge from my dazzled state before a voice addresses me. The person speaks in broken French. Perhaps not as broken as all that. His accent makes me think that he must be a German-speaker. He must be a German-speaking Swiss.

'Your papers, monsieur,' says the voice.

I slowly open my eyes, and I see two plain-clothes men. They're wearing badges on lanyards. They must be from the police.

'Why? What's going on?' I ask, waking up from my little nap.

'No questions, monsieur. Your papers.'

'Why are you only inspecting him?' ask the Santas sitting opposite me.

'One more word and we'll arrest the lot of you at the next stop,' they reply.

I calmly present my residence permit. They check it, make phone calls, no doubt to an office to verify my identity. Once that's done, they give me back my document, almost chucking it in my face. They move on without saying goodbye, without saying have a nice evening, without wishing us a merry Christmas.

My fellow passengers are gobsmacked. I don't have time to think about their shock. I pull my hood down over my face again and go back to sleep, hoping that this time I'll dream about Mama, that she'll say something to me, that she'll tell me at last what she's really feeling, that she'll open the gates to the world she's retreated to over the past two weeks.

23

At the end of my meeting with Monsieur Burioni in Lausanne, I feel an immense surge of joy. I have a job. At last! I have it, my very own job! I have a proper employment contract. I start on the first of January. It's all signed. I will be the PR officer of Monsieur Burioni, animal rights lawyer. He doesn't only defend animals, this Burioni. He also does wealth management. For years, he's helped the rich and famous hide their gombo under the mountains. But now he's convinced that the future of his business also lies in defending animal rights. And to help develop his plans, my job will be to find him new clients. I'll have to reach out to prospective customers. That's no problem for *me*! I'm used to it. Wasn't I a door-to-door sales rep for Monsieur Nkamba's beauty products?

Outside, a chill wind is gusting, making me feel even colder. On Place Saint-François, people are scuttling to and fro with the speed of sprinters. I feel like stopping them in their tracks. I wish I could shout out my happiness to them. I wish I could tell them not to worry about me any more. From now on, all is well. Very well, even. I smile at all the passers-by. I look completely mad, insane. I walk down Rue du Petit-Chêne, heading for the station, my steps keeping pace with the mellow

Christmas music. I stop and dance with a beggar who asks me for some change. Taken aback, he doesn't protest but dances with me. I give him a fat banknote. He can't believe his eyes. I continue on my way thinking of what I'll soon be earning.

How much will I be earning? Ooh, the gombo! Good gombo, nice and fresh. I start to feel intoxicated at the thought. How proud I'll be to run into Safia and Orphélie again! I'll have things to tell them. Monsieur Mazongo Mabeka, the social worker, I'll go and see him too, that horrible coconut. I'll hand him a letter of resignation from his benefits, from me and Ruedi. If we have to pay anything back, I'll do so, and with pleasure! I'll also make a point of going to see my unemployment adviser. I'll tell her how I managed to find work without her. She'll be pleased for me. I'll go and see Madame Bauer, Mireille Laudenbacher and Monsieur Khalifa, the three companions in the struggle. I'll tell them how grateful I am. Without them, I'd never have been able to land such a job. Not even in my dreams. I'll give Mireille Laudenbacher's dog a special present. He deserves it!

I'll go to the Grison mountains, to the Baumgartners' place, to thank them for their help. I know that Baumgartner père is a great red-wine lover. I'll give him a centuries-old grand cru. I'll also visit Kosambela in Lugano. She can book massage sessions on me, so no more backache.

I'll take my nephews Gianluca and Sangoh to the Circus Knie. I'll go to Bantuland, to M'fang and M'bangala. I'll buy baby clothes for my cousin

Ntoumba's baby. He'll join us here in Switzerland if he wants to leave his kid in Africa . . . and, best of all, I'll buy myself some new Louboutins. The very latest. The ones I saw recently in a window display in Rue du Rhône in Geneva. Everyone will know that something has happened in my life.

Everyone but Mama . . .

I phone Kosambela to tell her my news, but more importantly to find out if there's any change in Mama's condition.

'We must keep praying,' she says, after congratulating me.

'Yes. But what does Bernasconi say?'

'The nurses say they're doing their utmost to help her get better.'

'What about Bernasconi?'

She tells me that Docta Bernasconi is still very concerned even though he acknowledges that he's seen some little improvements in these past few hours. But that's not enough. Mama is still in a very unstable condition. A critical condition.

I'm one of those people who believe that one piece of good news leads to another. So, I prefer to stay calm. Mama will get better, I convince myself. Nzambe, Elolombi and the Bankoko can hear me.

Back at the apartment, I find Ruedi. He was waiting impatiently for me. He quizzes me with his eyes about my interview with Monsieur Burioni. I smile at him. He throws himself into my arms. I knew it! I knew it! he says. He's already laid the table. There are three place settings. The third person is Dominique. Ruedi invited him. He turned up with a fillet of beef as he'd promised me. Our little dining room is filled with the aroma of honey-roast beef and garlic. Ruedi puts on a relaxing Angélique Kidjo track to create an ambiance. No time to lose. We have to celebrate the good news. Our nightmare is over.

Just as we sit down to eat, my phone rings again. It's Kosambela.

'We haven't laid a place for you,' I say.

'Mwana . . .' she replies in a quavering voice.

'Hello! Hello, Kosambela? Is Monga Minga all right? Tell me, is Mama all right?'

'You have to come. Quickly. It's urgent.'

'What?!'

'The doctors. Mama.'

She sobs. I leap up from the table and shut myself in the bedroom.

'They say she's only got twenty-four hours left. It's over. She won't live much longer.'

'What?'

'You have to come, quickly.'

My heart's thudding. I can hear it pounding in my ears. Kidjo's music doesn't soothe me. My hands, my feet, my entire body is shaking like a leaf in the autumn wind. Tears well up in my eyes. I act tough, as usual. I must stay calm. But I'm rapidly defeated. My tears flow. They flow abundantly. I come out of the bedroom. Ruedi and Dominique are there, at the door. They want to know what's wrong. I am silent. I am lost.

I go into the bathroom and hastily wash my face. A wail of anguish is forming in my belly. I don't want to let it out. Ruedi strokes my back while Dominique stands in the doorway. I clench my teeth and try to hold down my wail. Shut up, Mwana. Shut up and control your body. I can't. I let out a howl of despair that fills the apartment. I cry from the depths of my being. I see the bad coming. I see death. I see Mama dead. Ruedi holds my shoulder. The tears won't stop streaming from my eyes. Grief is there. It trots painfully around my belly. A crown of headaches makes me dizzy.

Are you OK, *schätzli*? Ruedi asks. I have no answer. He must be panic-stricken. He starts to cry. What's going on? he asks. Tell me, what's going on? Ruedi's crying even harder than me. Dominique seems at a loss. He comes into the bathroom. He squeezes between us and holds us around the waist. He whispers sweet words. He comforts us. It'll be all right. It'll be all right. Mwana? Mwana, can you hear me? It'll be all right. Calm down, Ruedi. Everything will be OK.

'Calm down now,' both of you.

'Mama!!!' I howl.

'No, not that,' Ruedi's crying.

'Mama!!!' I howl again like a child seeking comfort in the arms of his absent mother.

'No, *schätzli*. Please, not that. No!'

'Yes. Any minute. Any minute now. Twenty-four hours . . .'

Only twenty-four hours. The doctor says she's only got twenty-four hours.

Dominique too is stunned by what I've just announced. He still has his arms around our waists and is trying to soothe us. In his whispered voice as he does his utmost to comfort us, I can hear his tears. He asks Ruedi to fetch my coat. Ruedi doesn't budge. You have to go to Lugano right away, Dominique tells me. I'll come with you, says Ruedi. I dart him a look that makes him change his mind. It's not the best time to meet Kosambela. Dominique and Ruedi hug me. Be brave, Dominique says. Slowly, he manages to extricate me from Ruedi's embrace. He steers Ruedi into the bedroom. Emerges a few moments later and offers to come with me to Cornavin railway station.

I jump on the first train. Destination Lugano. It's a six-hour journey. Long enough to empty me of my tears and perhaps leave some of my grief on the tracks, on the ticket inspectors, on some passengers, in the landscapes of the Swiss countryside that I'll pass through and also on the fat cows placidly grazing on the green grass in the meadows. I'll leave some of my grief at all the stations I pass through. That's what I'll do. I'll deposit pieces of my grief here and there along my way.

In the train, I do nothing but cry. My hiccups aren't so noisy, but not very discreet either. Between Berne and Zurich, two old ladies come and sit opposite me. They quickly realise that I'm in a bad way. Their faces show their sympathy. They seem to have compassion for me. One of them holds out a packet of tissues. That's helpful, I've run out. I take one and blow my nose noisily. Oh!

mutters one of the two old women wearing a pink puffa jacket. The other one is in a roll-necked pullover. I allow myself to give a little smile. These ladies haven't taken their eyes off me throughout the journey. They gave me a banana, two chocolate-filled biscuits and two packets of tissues. Thank you, *viel mal*, I managed to whisper.

Throughout the journey to Lugano, I received comforting messages from several passengers even though they knew nothing about the source of my sorrows. In my bag, at the end of the journey, I have a store of little gifts: a nice, yellow banana, two chocolate-filled biscuits, five packets of tissues, an apple, a bottle of water and even a spliff! That's right, a spliff given to me by a youth. He said: have this, it'll cheer you up. By the end of my journey, I've got loads of treats, but not even a tiny slice of life I could give my mother. A slice of life, of breath, real breath that I could breathe into her mouth to prolong her life even for a few minutes.

24

The snow on the ground hampers my progress. From the bottom of the hill up to San Salvatore hospital, I can hear a strange noise. It sounds like ululations, or rather wailing. It turns out to be wailing. Between sobs, I can at last recognise Auntie Botonghi's voice. She got there before me. She must have driven.

A few metres from the hospital, I spot a group of women in traditional pagnes from our country. They are also wearing headscarves. They've congregated in the foyer of the hospital's main entrance: Auntie Botonghi and four other women who I don't know. They're sitting on the floor and shedding all the tears in their bodies. One of them, as large as a hippopotamus, is rolling on the floor. She won't let the cold stop her from upholding her good Bantu ways. She wails: Nzambe, aie! Nzambe, aie! How can you allow such a thing?! Why her, aie, Nzambe?! Why Monga Minga? Lying on her back, the plump woman bangs her feet on the floor.

A security guard tries to move them away. He is closely followed by a receptionist, who looks completely shocked. The ladies in traditional pagnes don't pay them the least attention. They carry on weeping – as is fitting. As is done back home.

When Auntie Botonghi sees me, she yells loudly, Mwana!!! She bursts into tears and now she's rolling on the floor too. She raises her hands to the heavens. My son Mwana! Why has Nzambe done this to us? I feel my heart begin to pound. What has Nzambe done to us? Didn't Bernasconi say she still had twenty-four hours? My auntie carries on rolling on the floor close to the hippopotamus lady. I go over to them and try to calm them down. They fight me off. As I try to pull their multi-coloured pagnes over their exposed behinds, I notice, across the foyer, near the Christmas tree occupying pride of place in the main waiting room, a group of Manager-Sisters and gawkers. They seem nonplussed by what they are witnessing. One sister makes the sign of the cross and another moves her lips. She must be praying.

Kosambela joins us. Her eyes are red. She's holding her rosary. She's serene. I've never seen her so serene. When the mourners see her, they go rushing over to her and throw themselves at her feet. In a controlled, steady voice, Kosambela asks them to calm down. She doesn't add a single word. Auntie Botonghi and the other women gradually fall silent. Some of them adjust their headscarves. Others look for their sandals flung several dozen metres away in their panic.

When they are all quiet, Kosambela directs them to the waiting room on the fourth floor, where Mama is living her final hours.

Kosambela speaks: 'My mothers, we must thank God in all things. His will is not always ours. If He has decided this, then we must simply say amen.'

A lady bursts out sobbing anew. She wants to throw herself to the floor. Auntie Botonghi restrains her. Not here, sister, she says. The lady controls herself.

'Can I see my sister one last time?' asks Auntie Botonghi.

Kosambela replies that she must simply conduct herself appropriately. She reminds them of the regulations they must follow before going into Mama's room. You have to wear gloves, a mask, a gown, plastic overshoes and so on. Because Mama is still alive. True, she only has a few hours. But she's still alive. And while she's alive, there's still hope.

My sister shows them into Mama's room one at a time. When they come out, they're distraught. They are consumed with grief. One of them says she didn't recognise Mama. My sister looks like a dead corpse, she says through her sobs. Each one comes out with her comments, her observations and her tears. Auntie Botonghi is sitting on the floor, right beside the door of room 415. She hugs her knees to her chin. She'll spend the night there. She tells me so when I go over to comfort her. She asks me to be strong. She and the other ladies will sleep in the waiting room, on the other side.

'Who are these mothers here with you?' I ask her.

'They're women from the village in M'bangala, except Mafuta, the very very fat one, who comes from M'fang. I know the Bantu women of Geneva through our auntie. They decided to come and mourn their sister with me.'

'But Auntie, have they ever met Mama?'

'My son Mwana, do you have to know the dead person to mourn them?'

I am in Mama's room, sitting in a chair with casters. This is where I'm going to spend the night, waiting for Mama's final hour. At the last minute, I drop off. On the other side of the room is Kosambela. She's keeping watch. She mutters her prayers non-stop. Her neck is rigid and her eye vigilant. She's watching over Mama's body. Her body is lying there. Bernasconi informed us earlier that there was no longer any hope. He told us there was no point keeping her alive in this way. He said that over the past few days, he and his team had been simply keeping her alive. They couldn't allow it to go on. Did he need to remind us that Mama was there thanks to charity? Did he need to remind us how much it costs to repatriate a body to Bantuland? A friendly word of advice, he said, it would be better to switch off her life support now and send her home very quickly so that she could spend her final moments among her loved ones. He told us that there wasn't much time to lose thinking about it. We should do it now. While she's still alive.

Kosambela said no. We'll keep her on life support. We'll keep her alive as long as possible. Even if we get into debt. Kosambela told Bernasconi that she would sell her soul and her children to save her mother.

As for me, I had nothing to add. When Kosambela makes her mind up, that's how it is. No one will make her change her decision.

She tells her beads. From time to time, I gaze at the crucifix hanging just above Mama's head and close to the painting of the Virgin whose son refuses to grow up. What if my sister had made the wrong decision? What if we had to keep Mama in this state for a long time? And what if she had to remain in an induced coma for years? I'm the one who'd have to fork out for it. Because I have a good job now. I earn good gombo now. But would I want to spend all my gombo only to see my mother lying there, dead, living-dead, in a hospital bed? Is that really what I want? Deep down, an inner voice is pushing me to bow to the inevitable, to give in. That voice, in the depths of my consciousness, is speaking to me. It's telling me to go and talk to Kosambela and ask her to go back on her decision. No, you know your sister will never agree. Go and see Bernasconi instead. Go and find him. Talk to him. Talk man to man, educated men, intellectuals, and even as gay men. He'll understand you. He'll see how reasonable you are, and less fanatical. Go and talk to him.

I rise from my chair on casters and head towards the door.

'Where are you going?' asks Kosambela.

'I'm going to stretch my legs.'

'This is not the time.'

'I'm going to the toilet.'

'I said this is not the time.'

I go back to my seat. I gaze at my gloved hands and the rest of the trappings I'm wearing. Is that how I want to continue seeing my mother? Rubber gloves, a gown, a cap, and all that? I get up. I go over to Mama's inert body. She really is unrecognisable. I'm not able to cry any more. Even if she were to die, I don't think I'd be able to cry over her body. I've run out of tears. I'm all wrung out. And besides, I think there are deaths over which there's no point crying. Those who've made you suffer with them. I've spent the past four months crying all the time. I've spent four months hoping for a miracle. Because Bernasconi had told us from the beginning. He'd told us that Mama's cancer was terminal. That he and his team would do what they could. That even if she survived, her life wouldn't be as it was before. She would have severe after-effects. She wouldn't be able to eat normally again. All her food would have to be mashed up. Even simple bananas. Yoghurt would have to be diluted, then strained through a cloth. Is that the mother I'd want to have with me in the future? Would she be a mother or an infant?

Kosambela carries on praying. She doesn't cry.

She doesn't cry. She keeps an open Bible beside Mama's bed. She mutters. Then she speaks. I can hear her: How? How can you allow such a thing? Oh Nzambe! You, the God of our souls! You, the God of our ancestors! How can you allow such a shameful thing! What will our brothers and sisters, fathers and mothers in Bantuland think? What will they think of this? Will they still believe in Your name? And even if it matters little to you whether they believe in Your name or not, think about Bernasconi's efforts. Those villagers must continue to believe in the White man's medicine, in human medicine. Did not You, O Great Nzambe, give man the intelligence to cure your children? So why are you doing this?

My sister is speaking to Nzambe, Elolombi and the Bankoko, the ancestors. Now she chides Sangoh, our father. And what about you, Papa! What about you, Pa! What are you doing up there? Did you go up there to sleep? What about our military protection that you tore away from us all of a sudden? . . . Did you think about that? . . . Oh, yes, I understand. You loved Auntie Botonghi more! Yes, that's it. You loved her more than Monga Minga. Otherwise, how can you explain why you have always watched over Auntie Botonghi? She was able to come to Switzerland whereas Mama had to suffer all the fury of the M'fang villagers. Mama lost all her possessions. She had to start all over again among the M'bangala. But as for Auntie Botonghi, she's lived a nice-nice life here, among the White people.

She breaks off. She tells her beads once more and reties her headscarf.

But you listen to me, Sangoh. Listen carefully, I say. A true-true soldier doesn't make the same mistake twice. I know you know that. I say that a true-true soldier can't make the same mistake twice. Unless he's a complete idiot. *Ô né tit?* Are you an idiot? I don't believe you. Here's your wife. Here's Monga Minga. If you were able to speak with Elolombi and Nzambe to help her come here to Switzerland for treatment, go on, speak to them now and ask them to let her live. I'm telling you to do it. Just do as I ask and then you and I can talk afterwards.

Kosambela believes in our holy Trinity: Nzambe, Elolombi and Bankoko. She still has faith in it. I, on the other hand, have always been sceptical in the face of this merry-go-round of beliefs. But tonight, powerlessness forces me to face up to the facts. If Bernasconi and his team can't do any more, perhaps our Trinity can do something. Yes, something, but what? What can they do in such a critical situation? And if they'd been able to do something, they should have done it sooner, shouldn't they! They should have stopped this vile disease from getting into Mama's throat. And what disease? Cancer! Can we, true-true Bantu people, can we also suffer from it? Even with my Master's and my position as PR and communications manager for Monsieur Burioni's law firm, I've always been convinced that cancer was a disease only of the rich. Of the rich and the White people; in other words, a disease of the Whites. That's right, a disease of the White people because me, despite all the gombo that will come to me when I start work as communications manager, I don't imagine myself for one moment suffering from cancer. No. I'm Black, I am. Cancer's not for us Blacks.

My phone rings. Kosambela glares at me. It's Ruedi. I don't pick up. I put the phone on vibrate. A few minutes later, it vibrates. It's Dominique now, trying to get hold of me. Again, I don't answer. I'll be in touch tomorrow morning, I message them.

25

Ruedi and I are in Klosters, in the Grisons. We decided to take a trip to the mountains. You have to cross the vast white mantle covering the region to get to Carmils, at an altitude of two thousand metres. It's a beautiful, relaxing place, Ruedi said. After everything we've been through, we deserve a pleasant break.

I've been in my new job in Monsieur Burioni's law firm for a month. It's all going very well. More than very well. Monsieur Burioni is amazed at my powers of persuasion. In one month, I've brought in a dozen clients. The ones who complain about masters who abandon their dogs without bothering to remove their ID chip. Those who suspect their neighbours of cruelty towards their pets. Those who are shocked by people who acquire a four-legged animal when they're not able to take them for even the briefest walk. Those whose dog is in danger of being put down because it barely scratched a spoiled brat who was taunting it. These are all the people I've brought into Burioni's practice.

I've now had my first pay cheque and my first bonuses. In a few months' time, Ruedi and I will move to a new apartment. We'll find a bigger one. Much bigger. We intend to live with Dominique. He's a good guy. A trouple – that can't be so bad.

I met Madame Bauer and company to thank them. I gave Mireille Laudenbacher's dog a tuxedo. Here, in Klosters, I gave Monsieur Baumgartner a very special bottle of vintage wine. As I'd anticipated, my adviser at the unemployment office was very happy to learn that I'd landed something. I still haven't seen Safia or Orphélie since getting the job. They're bound to be on Facebook. I'm going to create an account, and who knows, perhaps I'll end up finding them online. I'll tell them my news.

Madame Baumgartner promised to teach me Swiss-German. She says it'll help me canvass clients in the German-speaking regions of Switzerland too. Then she adds another argument.

'With Schweizerdeutsch, you'll be able to become a . . . a . . .' She hesitates. She doesn't know the word in French. She turns to her son to ask for his help. '*Also Ruedi, wiä säit mä Eidgenosse uf französisch?*' she asks in an accent typical of her valley.

'That means, a real Swiss person. A real Swiss person born and bred.'

'With Schweizerdeutsch, you'll be able to become a real Swiss person, born *und bret*,' she says.

'Like Monsieur Mazongo Mabeka,' concludes Ruedi, laughing.

As for Monsieur Baumgartner, he promised to buy me snowshoes. He even promised to teach me how to ski. A real Swiss person must be at home in the mountains.

But while awaiting this process of becoming Swiss, I can bring out my Bantu flag. I attach it to my backpack. Ruedi and I set off for Carmils at an altitude of two thousand metres. He's lent me a pair of snowshoes. We plod slowly on, hampered by the snow. We cross breathtaking landscapes that there's no point describing, or painting. You just need to go there and see them with your own eyes. Once in a corner of Carmils, we sit down on a big rock. We'll eat our dinner here: slices of bread and butter with Gruyère.

'Look in front of you,' Ruedi says. 'That peak there is the Casanna.'

The sight does not leave me indifferent. I gaze at the snow-capped peaks. Shapes glide across the landscape. They're skiing.

'Over there, to the right, is the Madrisa, almost three thousand metres high. Then, to the left is the Gatschiefer. Its rock is magnificent.'

Ruedi tells me that the Casanna almost has cult status in the area. It's like a god. Legend has it that in this peaceful area, this beautiful place, there once lived a charming lady. She's said to have turned an over-inquisitive and disbelieving man to stone. He shows me what are supposedly the remains of the man turned to stone. I laugh. I tell him about my Bantu Trinity. We talk about our peoples' legends and beliefs. We don't believe in these things. Even so, we think they're important, especially at difficult and testing moments.

Kosambela was right to have faith in the Bantu Trinity. Mama is well and truly alive. She's still in San Salvatore hospital. But she's no longer connected to any tubes. According to Bernasconi, she'll be ready to be discharged in a few weeks. Perhaps at the end of March.

Or even before. Kosambela says that her gods did not forsake her. She says that Nzambe performs miracles. The Manager-Sisters respect her even more. She'll be promoted to head of the cleaning section. That means a little pay rise. But that's not all. The Manager-Sisters decided to give us a ten per cent reduction on the final bill. What happened is exceptional, they said.

No one believed it was possible. I remember that terrible night when I was in Mama's room, waiting for the end. We waited for a long time. Sleep got the better of our resolve. We dozed off like weary disciples on the Mount of Transfiguration. But we hadn't slept for long. At daybreak, I found Kosambela asleep, her mouth open and her rosary in her hand. I woke her. Gently. She gave a start. Together, we went slowly over to Mama's body. Kosambela rubbed her eyes hard. She muttered something that I couldn't hear, even though I was very close to her. Perhaps she was praying again. Perhaps she was preparing to curse our Bankoko. I had eyes only for Mama. I held her right forefinger, hoping for another message. She opened her eyes. Feebly. She closed them again then opened them once more. Oh Nzambe! my sister whispered. Are you feeling all right? I asked Mama in a voice filled with emotion. She waggled her right forefinger. Kosambela and I were in tears. Mama smiled at us with that smile that only we, her children, could see. I embraced Kosambela. I'd had faith. She would live. Bernasconi's twenty-four hours weren't yet up. But there was more hope than ever. That day was a little like what I see now in front of me, the beautiful Grison mountains which demand silence and awe, for sure, but which also give you a real reason to hope.

'Mwana,' Ruedi calls me. 'You know, one day, I'll take you over there. You see over there? That's the Gotschna, over two thousand metres high. The rocks there are red. They're so beautiful.'

Glossary

bangala	penis
Eidgenosse	Swiss citizen
gombo	money
kongolibon	shaven head
pagne	a length of fabric wrapped around the hips
plantain	euphemism for penis
tchop	food